PET STORIES FOR CHILDREN

ff

PET STORIES
FOR
CHILDREN

edited by
Sara and Stephen Corrin

Illustrated by Jill Bennett

faber and faber
LONDON · BOSTON

First published in 1985
by Faber and Faber Limited
3 Queen Square, London WC1N 3AU
Printed in Great Britain by
Redwood Burn Limited
Trowbridge, Wiltshire.

British Library Cataloguing in Publication Data
Pet stories for children.
I. Corrin, Sara II. Corrin, Stephen
823'.01'089282[J]   PZ7

Library of Congress Cataloging in Publication Data
Corrin, Sara.
Pet stories for children.

Summary: A collection of stories about pets ranging
from cats, dogs, and ponies to goats, giraffes, and
ravens.
1. Children's stories, English. [1. Pets – Fiction.
2. Animals – Fiction. 3. Short stories] I. Corrin,
Stephen. II. Bennett, Jill, ill. III. Title.
PZ5.C778Pe 1985   [Fic]   85–4413

ISBN 0–571–13642–7 (pbk.)

CONTENTS

for Tom
and for Juliet, whose idea it was

PETS – OUR KITH AND KIN

The love of pets seems to be almost universal. Most of us have either owned a pet ourselves or been close to someone who owned one, and the sheer variety of creatures kept as pets is staggering. A nephew of ours used to confide in his pet goldfish and was deeply distressed when it died. We have a newspaper cutting about a fish called Snoopy, which was saved by the kiss of life; Janet, Snoopy's young owner, sucked out the stone caught in his gills and had it set in her bracelet as a souvenir.

At first a child longs just for *a* pet, but once the pet has settled down in the home *a* becomes *my* and no substitute will do. No one writes more understandingly of a child's intense relationship with his pet than Meindert de Jong. In *Shadrach* he describes young Davie's dismay and bewilderment when his parents suggest getting him another black rabbit – just the same kind – after his own is lost. To Davie the idea is inconceivable. It's Shadrach and only Shadrach, not just *any* old black rabbit, that he wants. In that exquisitely beautiful story *A Horse Came Running*, by the same author, Mark is told by his father that really his old horse, Colonel, would be better off dead. "They just don't understand," thinks Mark. "Better off? He'd be dead, wouldn't he?" He feels that his horse returns his affection. Colonel is his friend, *he* understands him. These two wonderful stories are too long for inclusion in this anthology, but no animal-lover should miss the thrill of reading them.

Both adults and children have been known to risk their lives to rescue their dogs, while dogs can become obsessively attached to their owners. Have you ever watched a dog tethered outside a shop, shivering in every sinew, eyes bent on the door through which his owner has disappeared and waiting only for his return? But it is not just a pet's dependence on us that evokes feelings of responsibility and loving care. The question is: who owns whom? Perhaps *we* follow our dog, although he is on a lead. "It's funny, my puppy/Knows just how I feel./When I'm happy/He's yappy . . ." writes Aileen Fisher. What strikes one about a dog is that you can *always* count on its unswerving love and loyalty, whatever others may think of you, or even if you do the most stupid things (as we all do from time to time).

A pet is not just a cuddly toy; he has his own nature, as the child intuitively realizes. "You can't pick up Silky (the cat) just when *you* fancy. Silky's got to fancy *you*. She'll find her own comfy position and then she'll enjoy your stroking," said eight-year-old Tom to his grandma.

Our stories come from many countries and the pets range from the familiar cat, dog, hamster and pony to a goat, a kangaroo, a giraffe and a jackdaw. Joan Aiken's inimitable raven Mortimer is perhaps the most amusing, and the oddest is surely the crocodile which appears in *Katya, the Crocodile and the School Pets*.

SAM BECOMES . . . A GHOST!

John Cunliffe

All week I had begged and begged Granny to take me to Blackpool Fun-Fair. Granny didn't like fairs, I knew, but I also knew that if I kept on long enough, nagging about it, she would give in at last and take me. It was only a matter of time and patience. I was just beginning to think that she wasn't going to give in this time, when she did.

"Oh, all right, then," she said, "we'll go this afternoon; but think on — once your money's spent you're not getting any more. You can only spend it once."

I was instantly fizzing with excitement, and I was ready to agree to any conditions. All I wanted was to blow all the money I could lay hands on, for a glorious afternoon on the fun-fair.

"Yippeeeeee . . ." I shouted. "Thanks, Granny, dear! Hurrah, we're going to the fair!"

I took Sam by the front paws, and danced him all round the caravan, until Granny said, "Now calm down, or we'll not go to the blessed fair. Now I've told you, the two of you; stop it, or else . . . you're going to tip the whole bag of tricks over."

The caravan was beginning to rock dangerously, so I sat down and tried as well as I could to hold in my excitement. Sam sat at my feet, panting, watching Granny's every movement, and wondering why we'd been told off. There seemed such ages of time to get through before the afternoon came,

1

that I just didn't know how I was going to be able to wait.

One of Granny's favourite sayings was "Possess thy soul in patience". She kept saying this as the morning dragged on, and she saw that I was more and more restless. It didn't help at all; it made me even worse. I just *couldn't* possess my soul in patience, whatever that meant, and it only irritated me when she kept on saying it. Sam seemed to have caught my restless feeling, because he was restless, too. He kept running in and out of the caravan, and digging in the sand underneath it. Suddenly, there was a lurch, and the caravan tipped over to one side alarmingly. Granny and I ran outside. Sam had dug a deep hole just where one of the props held the caravan level, and the prop had dropped down into the hole. We had to move the caravan clear of the hole, and Granny smacked

Sam, and tied him up for the rest of the morning. I got through the morning somehow. I walked along the beach; I aimed pebbles at an old can; I ate an ice-cream; I joined in a game of beach football. Up to now, I'd enjoyed doing all these things, but suddenly they had all become boring. All I wanted was to get to the fair. Everything between now and the moment of arriving at the fair was just filling in time. Even dinner; it was a lovely dinner, with ice-cream and jelly to finish with; even dinner was a bore, and I hardly ate any at all. I only ate what I did because Granny said, "No dinner; no fair."

At last the great moment came. I had gathered up every last penny of my pocket-money, and begged some extra from Granny. I had put my clean clothes on. Sam had been brushed and combed, and put on a new lead. Granny had put her best hat on, and the new coat she had bought at Marks and Spencers. We looked really smart. All my feelings of boredom had dropped away. The whole world was bright and shining again, as we walked smartly along the road to the fairground. Then, when I saw the Big Dipper racing above the roofs of the houses, my heart began to race, too; I would have run all the way, if Granny had not had a firm hold on my hand.

I had a wonderful time on the fair. I went on the round-abouts, the bumper-cars, the chair-o-planes, the motor-boats, the switchback slide and the go-karts. I went in the Noah's Ark, and the maze of a thousand mirrors, and the Fun House. I didn't go on the Big Dipper – no, I never dared to go on that, though I stood and stood watching it, almost daring, wishing I could, longing to go on it, sometimes stepping up to the cash-desk with my money, then drawing back again, not having quite the courage. It was so high, and so fast, and so exciting; the people screamed as they went over the highest part, and plunged down at great speed, to swoop up again with a heart-sickening lurch towards the sky.

"Never mind," said Granny, "you'll be able to go on it when you're a bit older. Next year, perhaps."

But I never did. I just didn't have that amount of daring.

And then we came to the ghost-train! Now this was a different story altogether – oh, yes. This was something else that I had never before dared to go on. I had often seen them on travelling fairs at home. My friends had gone on them, and come out laughing and screaming, and sometimes looking a bit scared beneath the fun. Time and again they had tried to persuade me to go on the ghost-train with them, but it was no good – I just wouldn't. They had called me "cissy" and "chicken" but it made no difference; I would not, or could not, and that was that. But today was different; today I thought I might feel old enough and brave enough for the ghost-train. Besides, there were no friends to tease me and call me names, or to make fun of me if I came out looking really scared; there was just Granny, and she would be nothing but kindness to me. Oh, yes, and there was Sam of course. He had been very good as we had gone round the fair. He had sat patiently with Granny, and watched with some astonishment in his eyes, as I had whirled round and round, or whizzed through the air above his head. He clearly thought that I had gone quite mad, to want to do such things. But he would give me such a welcome that I would forget any frights on the ghost-train, I felt sure. Yes, I would go on the ghost-train, specially as it was so much bigger and better than the ones on the fairs at home, with real signals, flashing-lights, and strange shrieks and noises coming from the depths of its mysteriously dark tunnels. This would be something to boast about when I went home; something to show just how brave I had really grown to be. There was a small snack-bar near to the ghost-train, so Granny said she would go and have a cup of tea, and rest her poor old legs whilst I went for the ride. And, she said,

"Poor old Sam's been on his lead all afternoon, and he's been so very good. I'll just let him off for a bit, and give him a drop of tea in a saucer. He must be parched."

"Won't you come on the ghost-train with me, Granny?" I said. "I'll pay for you." (I must admit, I *was* a bit scared.)

"Never in this world," said Granny, "I'm too old for any

ghost-trains. No, you'll have to go on your own, or not at all. Now, if you're really too scared . . ."

But I wasn't going to let her persuade me away from it. No fear!

"Oh no, Granny, I'm not scared," I said, and off I went.

I had to queue for a while, to get my ticket, and I could see Granny in the snack-bar, with Sam lapping up his tea with great relish. Then I saw Sam looking round to see where I'd got to, and Granny pointing at me. I knew that she'd be telling him that I was all right, and would come back soon; all the same, Sam looked worried about what he considered my sudden disappearance. Why wasn't John sitting down with Granny, for a cup of tea? he seemed to be asking. Then he spotted me getting into the carriage of the ghost-train. This was too much for Sam. He must have decided that I needed rescuing from this most dreadful of all the machines he had seen that day. Before Granny could stop him, he hared across the space between the snack-bar and the ghost-train, jumped two walls and, just as the carriage jerked into motion, landed on the seat beside me, barking joyfully and licking his hot wet tongue all over my face. We sped into the darkness together in this manner. Now Sam decided he didn't like this at all, and set up the most dismal howling, which terrified everyone within earshot, and was far worse than anything the makers of the ghost-train had been able to invent. A girl in the carriage in front burst into tears, and I heard a man shouting something about werewolves.

"Shut up, Sam!" I shouted. "Don't be so *silly* – quiet, boy, it's only a ghost-train!"

But it was no good; the more loudly I shouted at him, the more loudly Sam howled.

"It's only a dog!" I shouted into the darkness, but my only answer was a shriek from the machinery, that set Sam off again. There was nothing I could do, but cling on to the carriage sides and try to keep hold of Sam. The carriage suddenly lurched round a sharp corner, making me lose my

grip on Sam. At the same moment a huge monster, glowing with green light, rose up in front of us, and opened its blood-stained jaws, as though it would swallow us. Sam took one look, and sprang at it, growling ferociously and with his teeth bared. He sank his teeth into the monster's plastic leg, and pulled it off. He was going back into the attack again as my carriage whirled me away into the darkness; I could hear Sam's battle, going farther and farther into the distance. What could I do? It was far too dangerous for me to jump out and try to catch Sam, as I could easily be run down in the darkness by the next carriage. I could only sit tight, and hope Sam wouldn't be hurt. I heard shouts from the following carriage, as they came upon Sam's battle, urging Sam on to victory.

6

"Go on, boy! Kill it! Shake it! Hurrah!

Then there were yells and screams, though I couldn't tell whether Sam or the ghost-train was causing them. Good as it was, there was nothing in that ghost-train to equal Sam. When I came out at the other end, Sam was nowhere to be seen, but a variety of howling and barking was coming from the darkness inside. Granny was talking to the men in charge. When I told them what had happened, one of them said, "We'll have to shut the whole thing down and go in with torches to get the dog out; but we cannot do that until everyone else is out."

One by one, the carriages came out into the daylight. Some of the people were laughing. Some looked really scared. Two little girls were crying. There was a babble of excited talk: people telling their stories about what had happened, as they gathered on the platform. One couple had been sitting in their carriage in the dark, when a large hairy animal had suddenly jumped on them, breathed hot air in their faces, and licked their hands, then jumped out again. They were so terrified that they'd sat as though frozen – unable to move or shout. Something like this had happened to quite a number of people. Sam must have gone from carriage to carriage, looking for me. Some had seen Sam's eyes glowing horribly in the darkness, and a lady had seen him running off down a tunnel with the monster's leg in his jaws. Everyone had their Sam story, and never before had that ghost-train been so scary!

At last, everyone was out, and the men switched all the machinery off. Then, with large torches glowing, four of them went into the tunnel, to look for Sam. The men disappeared from view, and we all waited, listening hard. A mixture of sounds came out.

"Jack! Jack! Over here! Can you shine your light over there? Look out . . . what's that? Damn! Look where you're going!"

All this grew fainter, as the men went farther in. The men went in at one end, and something came out at the other end,

7

but it wasn't our Sam, or it didn't, at first, look like Sam.

"Look!" shouted a man.

Looking into the dark tunnel, we all saw a luminous skeleton, and it was *moving*! It moved in a curious way, lying sideways a little way above the ground, with its arms and legs dangling, and shaking about. A number of people turned tail, and ran for it. They had had enough of frights. But, as the strange sight came out into the daylight, it turned out to be not at all frightening. The skeleton's strange movements were soon explained. It was being carried along in Sam's mouth, with its arms and legs dangling down on either side. As Sam trotted along, the skeleton danced about in a most ghoulish way.

"Come on, Sam, you silly boy," said Granny. But Sam had no intention of coming on, or of giving up his prize. He jumped over the wall, dragging the skeleton with him.

"Stop that dog! He's got our skeleton!" shouted a man. Dozens of people jumped over the wall and went after Sam, but Sam had seen them, and he was putting on speed now, across the fairground, with the skeleton waving frantically, as though beckoning on the pursuers. Granny and I followed on as fast we could, but we knew there would be no catching Sam once he'd got the bit between his teeth, as they say; or the skeleton, as it was in Sam's case. Out of the fairground Sam ran, and straight through the middle of a shopping-precinct. Here Sam caused great consternation, as the people didn't know he had taken the skeleton from a fair, and it did look realistic. Crowds gathered and stared. Two women fainted. A policeman began talking urgently into his radio. Sam ran in through the store, scattering shoppers right and left, and out at the other side. Now he had shaken off many of his pursuers, as they had become caught up in the crowds in Woolworth's, who had closed in behind Sam like the wake behind a ship. A few brave hearts kept Sam in view, though, as he turned along the sea-front, going as fast as ever. Even they lost him, when he suddenly turned into the road, and raced across in a suicide dash, between two trams, a double-decker bus, a ten-ton lorry, and a horse-carriage, missing them all by inches.

The skeleton waved farewell as Sam disappeared among the traffic, leaving the ghost-train men fuming on the pavement. By the time the traffic-lights stopped the traffic, and they could cross, Sam was nowhere to be seen.

The rest of the crowd wandered off home in twos and threes, but Granny and I went on looking for Sam for a long time. We didn't find him. Granny said,

"We'll have to go back to the fair, and ask how much we owe for the damage. I'm fair dreading it; I'll never be able to pay for all that dog's done today. Sam will be the ruination of me, yet."

But when we went to see the owner of the ghost-train, he was all smiles. "It's all right, missus, you don't need to pay a penny," he said. "We had a piece of luck, you see. Somebody rang the television people up about Sam and the skeleton, because they thought it made such a funny story. So they're sending a film-crew to interview us, and show the ghost-train and the damage. We'll be famous when we've been on telly. Everybody will want to ride on our train. It's marvellous free publicity. We're grateful to you – we really are."

"Well, then, that's a relief," said Granny.

"There's just one thing," the man said.

"What's that?"

"If you do find your dog, and he still has our skeleton . . . well, we would like the skeleton back. They're hard to get, and it is a good one."

"Certainly," said Granny, "but I cannot promise anything, knowing our Sam. He might have eaten it, whatever it's made of."

We went back to our caravan, wondering if we would ever see Sam again. Perhaps he had been killed in another mad dash across the road.

"Poor Sam, I'll miss him, if we don't find him," said Granny sadly. "For all that he's a mischief, sometimes, I'm very fond of him."

As Granny opened the door, there was a snuffling under

9

the caravan, and who should crawl out on his belly, looking very much ashamed of himself, but our Sam! Granny instantly grabbed him, and gave him the good hiding he deserved. Sam took it bravely. Then Granny said, "Now, Sam, what did you do with that skeleton? Bones, Sam, bones . . . Show me . . . show me, Sam."

He knew quite well what she meant, but it was quite clear that he wasn't going to show us. Perhaps he had eaten it – plastic, wire, and all. Whatever the answer, Sam went to bed that night without any supper.

The next few days were very windy, and the sand began to blow about and drift amongst the caravans. It was some days later that there was a knock at our caravan door, and a man with a very odd message, and a suspicious look on his face, was standing there.

"Excuse me," he said, "but do you know what's under your caravan?"

"Sand, as far as I know," said Granny.

"Come and look," said the man.

Granny looked. Sticking up in the sand were the skull and rib-cage of a human skeleton!

"Oh," said Granny, "I think I know how *that* got there. It's

all right, it's only plastic; it isn't a real one. Here, I think I'd better tell you the whole story."

"Perhaps you better had," said the man. So he came in for a cup of tea, and Granny told him the story. It was all in the papers, as well as on television, so she could prove it. In the end, the man helped to dig the skeleton up, or what was left of it. Sam had eaten one leg and given up in disgust, then buried the rest. Perhaps he had hoped it would improve with keeping? They parcelled it up neatly, and the man offered to take it back to the fair for us.

The ghost-train man sent us a free ticket, to go on the ghost-train as often as we wanted, provided that we didn't bring Sam; but I didn't fancy it, after all that had happened.

THE FLOOD

Ruth Ainsworth

The shed was near the house. It was dark because it had only one small window, and that was covered with cobwebs. There were some tools in the shed, a spade and a rake and a hoe, and a pile of old sacks. There was something else as well, that not many people knew about. If you stood quite still in the shed, without moving a hand or a foot, you could hear the crackle of straw and perhaps a tiny cry.

The crackle of straw and the cry came from a box standing in a corner. In the box were a mother cat and her three new-born kittens. The cat's name was Minnie and her kittens were named One, Two, and Three. When they were big and could wash themselves and drink milk from a saucer, they would go to homes of their own. Then someone would give them proper names. But One, Two, and Three did very well to start with.

Sometimes a dog barked.

"What is that?" asked One, his little legs shaking.

"It is only Prince, the dog," purred Minnie. "He is taking care of us. He barks when he sees a stranger coming."

Sometimes a door banged.

"What is that?" mewed Two, shuddering like a jelly.

"It is only the wind blowing the door shut," purred Minnie. "Now the wind won't get into our snug bed."

12

Sometimes the coalman tipped the coal out with a sound like thunder.

"What is that?" cried Three, hiding her face in her mother's fur.

"It is only the coalman," purred Minnie. "His coal will make the kitchen fire blaze and burn. I will take you into the kitchen for a treat, when you are bigger, if you are very good."

A lady named Mrs Plum lived in the kitchen. She wore a white apron. Every day she brought Minnie's meal to her, in a blue dish. When Minnie had finished her food, the dish was as clean as if it had been washed.

One night, when the kittens were fast asleep, curled like furry balls beside their mother, a storm blew up. The door and window of the shed rattled. The rain fell in floods on the roof. There were terrible claps of thunder and bright, zig-zag flashes of lightning. Even Minnie felt frightened. The river ran at the

13

bottom of the garden, on the other side of the garden wall, and she could hear it roaring by. It sounded like a fierce, growling animal.

"What is wrong? What has happened?" mewed One, Two, and Three.

"I don't know, my dears," said Minnie. "But we must go to sleep and not be frightened."

But Minnie herself was very frightened and so were the three kittens. No one could get to sleep while the storm was raging.

The kittens were so young that their eyes were not yet open. But Minnie's eyes shone like green lamps. She could see, under the door of the shed, a trickle of water. The trickle grew into a puddle. The puddle grew into a wave. The wave came nearer and nearer across the floor. Then it reached the box in the corner.

Minnie did not like water. She did not even like getting her paws wet on the wet grass. She was very, very frightened to see the water creeping under the door and spreading across the whole floor.

"If it gets any deeper," she thought to herself, "I shall take the kittens in my mouth, one at a time, and jump on to the wheelbarrow, and then up on to the shelf where the flower-pots are stacked. I don't think the water could get as high as that."

The water flowed faster and faster under the door until it was inches deep. Just when Minnie was getting ready to take a kitten in her mouth and spring on to the wheelbarrow, and then on to the shelf, a strange thing happened. The wooden box began to move about. It was floating. It was floating like a boat.

There was a thick layer of straw in the bottom of the box and an old woollen jersey. The kittens stayed dry and warm while they floated in their bed. They did not mind at all because they could not see the water as their eyes were shut.

Suddenly there was a clap of thunder and a great blast of wind. The door of the shed blew open with a bang. The water

14

rushed in and the box swirled round and round. Then it floated out of the shed into the garden.

The river had risen so high that it swept over the garden wall. The box swished over the wall and sailed along the river which was now wide and deep like a sea. It was too dark to see exactly where they were going. Minnie cuddled her babies close to her while the rain fell in torrents. The kittens were soon fast asleep, and though Minnie was sure she would never get a wink herself, she dozed off as well.

When the morning came, they were in a watery world. There was water in front of them. Water behind. Water all round. Minnie had not known there could be so much water in one place. Strange things floated by. Branches of trees which had been torn off by the storm. Tables and chairs and pillows and cushions that had been washed out of houses. Sacks and straw and even a dog-kennel. Minnie was pleased to see that the kennel was empty.

Nothing stopped Minnie from bringing up her kittens as well as she could, so she washed them just as carefully as if they had been on dry land. When she had finished One's face, he mewed in an excited voice:

"I can see! I can see! I can see you and Two and Three and the water and everything!"

He frisked about with joy and Minnie was afraid he might fall out of the box.

Before long, Two and Three could see as well and they spent most of the day calling out:

"What's that? What's that? What's that?" or else: "Why is the water shiny? Why is it brown?" and many other questions, some of which Minnie could not answer.

Though the kittens were well and happy, Minnie was worried. The kittens were fat as butter and could drink her warm milk whenever they wished. But there was nothing for *her* to eat, no milk – no fish – no liver. Nothing at all.

The other thing that worried her was that she could not bring her children up properly in a box floating on the water. How would they learn to lap milk from a saucer? Or walk upstairs? Or climb trees? Or catch mice? Minnie had brought up so many families of kittens that she knew exactly how the job ought to be done.

Now that the rain had stopped the floods began to go down. The river was no longer wild and roaring. Hedges and bushes could be seen that had been under the water a few hours before. When the box drifted near the bank and was caught on the branches of a willow tree, Minnie knew what she must do.

Quick as a flash, she snatched up the nearest kitten, who happened to be Two, and climbed up the tree with him. She dashed back for One and Three and the little family were soon perched on the damp, slippery branch of a willow, instead of cuddled in a floating cradle filled with straw.

"This is a horrid place!" mewed One.

"I shall fall into the water and be drowned!" mewed Two.

"How are we to sleep without a bed?" mewed Three.

Minnie was not comfortable herself as she was trying to look after three young kittens as well as hold on, but she did not approve of grumbling.

"The river is going down," she said cheerfully. "Tomorrow or the next day I shall carry you home, one at a time, in my mouth. Till then, you must be good kittens and do what I tell you."

"Do you know the way home?" asked One. "We must have floated a long way in our wooden box."

Minnie was not certain that she *did* know the way, but she replied firmly:

"Of course I know the way. The river brought us here. I shall just follow the river and it will lead us home. Anyhow, all sensible cats know the way home. They never get lost."

All day and all night Minnie took care of her kittens. She fed them and washed them and sang to them, and when they slept she kept them from falling off the branch. When they were awake and wanted to play, she told them stories. She told them about the red kitchen fire that ate black coal. She told them about mice with long tails who lived in holes and were fun to chase. She told them about dear Mrs Plum and her white apron and her warm, comfortable lap.

When the *next* morning came, the river had gone right down. The ground was wet and muddy, but it was not under water. They could see the path running along the river bank.

"I shall take one of you home now," said Minnie.

"Take me!" "No, me!" "No, ME!" mewed the three kittens.

"I shall take Three first because she is the smallest," said Minnie. "Now, One and Two, be brave and sensible and hold on tightly."

"What will happen if we fall off?" asked One and Two.

"You would lose one of your nine lives," said Minnie. "Then you would have only eight left."

She took little Three in her mouth, climbed down the tree to the ground, and ran off along the river bank. She felt sure she was going the right way and that every step was bringing her nearer home. The wet mud was cold and nasty to her feet, but she did not mind. If only her three kittens were safe in front of the kitchen fire, she would never mind anything again!

17

Little Three squirmed and squiggled and seemed to get heavier and heavier. When at last Minnie padded slowly through the gate and up the path to the back door, she could hardly drag one foot after the other.

"Miaow! Miaow!" she cried as loudly as she could. "Miaow!"

In a second the door opened and there stood dear Mrs Plum in her white apron.

"Oh, Minnie! Minnie!" she cried, gathering Minnie and Three up in her arms, and not minding at all about the mud they left on her apron. "I thought I should never see you again!"

At first Minnie purred loudly and smiled, but she knew the job was not yet finished. She began to kick and struggle till Mrs Plum put her down on the floor. Then she ran to the back door and mewed for it to be opened.

"I know," said Mrs Plum. "I understand. You must go back for the others. Wait a moment and I will come too, I'll just make Three safe and comfortable. I kept a bed ready for you all."

There, on the hearth-rug, was another box with a soft blanket inside. Mrs Plum cuddled Three into the blanket, and Three sat and stared at the fire with round blue eyes. So *this* was the monster who ate black coal!

Mrs Plum put on her coat and hat and took a basket with a lid and opened the door. Minnie ran ahead so quickly that Mrs Plum could only just keep up. They were both tired when they got to the willow tree. Mrs Plum stood at the bottom while Minnie climbed up and found her two kittens cold and shivering, but quite safe.

"We've kept all our nine lives, Mother!" they called out.

"That's my good kittens!" said Minnie, carrying them down to the ground, where Mrs Plum stroked them and petted them and tucked them into the basket, which was lined with flannel. There was just room for Minnie as well. Then Mrs Plum carried the heavy basket home. She had to change hands when one arm ached.

When they were back in the warm kitchen, Mrs Plum gave Minnie a good meal. She had sardines and a dish of cornflakes and three saucers of milk. Then they all five settled down for a cosy afternoon by the fire. Mrs Plum knitted in her rocking chair, and the three kittens watched the red fire eating coal and stared at the brass rim of the fender and the plates on the dresser and all the other wonderful things.

They kept looking at Mrs Plum's ball of wool.

"I don't know why, but I should like to roll that ball of wool all over the floor," said One.

"So should I!" said Two and Three.

"That would be very naughty of you indeed," said Minnie. "But I wanted to do just the same when I was a kitten."

"And did you do it?" asked the three kittens.

"Yes, I'm afraid I did!" said Minnie.

She purred and smiled and dozed, as the clock ticked on the wall and the fire crackled and Mrs Plum clicked her knitting needles.

ARABEL'S RAVEN

Joan Aiken

On a stormy night in March, not long ago, a respectable taxi-driver named Ebenezer Jones found himself driving home, very late, through the somewhat wild and sinister district of London known as Rumbury Town. Mr Jones was passing the long, desolate piece of land called Rumbury Waste, when, in the street not far ahead, he observed a large, dark, upright object. It was rather smaller than a coalhod, but bigger than a quart cider-bottle, and it was moving slowly from one side of the street to the other.

Mr Jones had approached to within about twenty yards of this object when a motor-cyclist, with a pillion passenger, shot by him at a reckless pace and cutting in very close. Mr Jones braked sharply, looking in his rear-view mirror. When he looked forward again he saw that the motor-cyclist must have struck the upright object in passing, for it was now lying on its side, just ahead of his front wheels.

He brought his taxi to a halt. "Not but what I daresay I'm being foolish," he thought. "There's plenty in this part of town that's best left alone. But you can't see something like that happen without stopping to have a look."

He got out of his cab.

What he found in the road was a large black bird, almost two feet long, with a hairy fringe round its beak. At first he thought it was dead. But as he got nearer, it opened one eye slightly, then shut it again.

"Poor thing; it's probably stunned," thought Mr Jones.

His horoscope in the *Hackney Drivers' Herald* that morning had said, "Due to your skill, a life will be saved today." Mr Jones had been worrying as he drove home, because up till now he had not, so far as he knew, saved any lives that day, except by avoiding pedestrians recklessly crossing the road without looking.

"This'll be the life I'm due to save," he thought. "Must be, for it's five to midnight now," and he went back to his cab for the bottle of brandy and teaspoon he always carried in the tool-kit in case lady passengers turned faint.

It is not at all easy to give brandy to a large bird lying unconscious in the road. After five minutes there was a good deal of brandy on the cobbles, and some up Mr Jones's sleeve, and some in his shoes, but he could not be sure that any had actually gone down the bird's throat. The difficulty was that he needed at least three hands: one to hold the bottle, one to hold the spoon, and one to hold the bird's beak open. If he prised open the beak with the handle of the teaspoon, it was sure to shut again before he had time to reverse the spoon and tip in some brandy.

21

Suddenly a hand fell on Mr Jones's shoulder.

"Just what do you think you're doing?" inquired one of two policemen who had left their van and were standing over him.

The other sniffed in a disapproving manner. Mr Jones straightened slowly.

"I was just giving some brandy to this rook," he explained. He was rather embarrassed, because he had spilt such a lot of the brandy.

"Rook? That's no rook," said the officer who had sniffed. "That's a raven. Look at its hairy beak."

"Whatever it is, it's stunned," said Mr Jones. "A motorbike hit it."

"Ah," said the second officer, "that'll have been one of the pair who just pinched thirty thousand quid from the bank in the High Street. It's the Cash-and-Carat boys – the ones who've done a lot of burglaries round here lately. Did you see which way they went?"

"No," said Mr Jones, tipping up the raven's head, "but they'll have a dent on their bike. Could one of you hold the bottle for me?"

"You don't want to give him brandy. Hot sweet tea's what you want to give him."

"That's right," said the other policeman. "And an ice-pack under the back of his neck."

"Burn feathers in front of his beak."

"Slap his hands."

"Undo his shoelaces."

"Put him in the fridge."

"He hasn't got any shoelaces," said Mr Jones, not best pleased at all this advice. "If you aren't going to hold the bottle, why don't you go on and catch the blokes that knocked him over?"

"Oh, *they*'ll be well away by now. Besides, they carry guns. We'll go back to the station," said the first policeman. "And you'd better not stay here, giving intoxicating liquor to a bird, or we might have to take you in for loitering in a suspicious manner."

"I can't just leave the bird here in the road," said Mr Jones.

"Take it with you, then."

"Can't you take it to the station?"

"Not likely," said the second policeman. "No facilities for ravens there."

They stood with folded arms, watching, while Mr Jones slowly picked up the bird and put it in his taxi. And they were still watching as he started up and drove off.

So that was how Mr Jones happened to take the raven back with him to Number Six, Rainwater Crescent, N.W.3½, on a windy March night.

When he got home, nobody was up, which was not surprising, since it was after midnight. He would have liked to wake his daughter Arabel, who was fond of all birds and animals. But since she was quite young – she hadn't started school yet – he thought he had better not. And he knew he must not wake his wife Martha, because she had to be at work at

Round & Round, the gramophone shop in the High Street, at nine in the morning.

He laid the raven on the kitchen floor, opened the window to give it air, put on the kettle for hot sweet tea, and, while he had the match lit, burned a feather-duster under the raven's beak. Nothing happened, except that the smoke made Mr Jones cough. He saw no way of slapping the raven's hands or undoing its shoelaces, so he took some ice-cubes and a jug of milk from the fridge. He left the fridge door open because his hands were full, and anyway it usually swung shut by itself. With great care he slid a little row of ice-cubes under the back of the raven's neck.

The kettle boiled and he made the tea: a spoonful for each person and one for the pot, three in all. He also spread himself a slice of bread and fish-paste because he didn't see why he shouldn't have a little something as well as the bird. He poured out a cup of tea for himself and an egg-cupful for the raven, putting plenty of sugar in both.

But when he turned round, egg-cup in hand, the raven had gone.

"Bless me," Mr Jones said, "there's ingratitude for you! After all my trouble! I suppose he flew out of the window; those ice-cubes certainly did the trick quick. I wonder if it would be a good notion to carry some ice-cubes with me in the cab? I could put them in a vacuum flask – might be better than brandy if lady passengers turn faint . . ."

Thinking these thoughts he finished his tea (and the raven's; no sense in leaving it to get cold), turned out the light, and went to bed.

In the middle of the night he thought, "Did I put the milk back in the fridge?"

And he thought, "No I didn't."

And he thought, "I ought to get up and put it away."

And then he thought, "It's a cold night, the milk's not going to turn between now and breakfast. Besides, Thursday tomorrow, it's my early day."

So he rolled over and went to sleep.

24

Every Thursday Mr Jones drove the local fishmonger, Mr
Finney, over to Colchester to buy oysters at five in the
morning. So, early next day, up he got, off he went. Made
himself a cup of tea, finished the milk in the jug, never looked
in the fridge.

An hour after he had gone Mrs Jones got up and put on the
kettle. Finding the milk jug empty she went yawning to the
fridge and pulled the door open, not noticing that it had been
prevented from shutting properly by the handle of a burnt
feather-duster which had fallen against the hinge. But she
noticed what was inside the fridge all right. She let out a
shriek that brought Arabel running downstairs.

Arabel was little and fair with grey eyes. She was wearing a
white nightdress that made her look like a lampshade with
two feet sticking out from the bottom. One of the feet had a
blue sock on.

"What's the matter, Ma?" she said.

"There's a great awful *bird* in the fridge!" sobbed Mrs Jones.
"And it's eaten all the cheese and a blackcurrant tart and five

25

pints of milk and a bowl of dripping and a pound of sausages. All that's left is the lettuce."

"Then we'll have lettuce for breakfast," said Arabel.

But Mrs Jones said she didn't fancy lettuce that had spent the night in the fridge with a great awful bird. "And how are we going to get it out of there?"

"The lettuce?"

"The *bird*!" said Mrs Jones, switching off the kettle and pouring hot water into a pot without any tea in it.

Arabel opened the fridge door, which had swung shut. There sat the bird, among the empty milk bottles. There was a certain amount of wreckage around him – torn foil, and cheese wrappings, and milk splashes, and bits of pastry, and crumbs of dripping, and rejected lettuce leaves. It was like Rumbury Waste after a picnic Sunday.

Arabel looked at the raven, and he looked back at her.

"His name's Mortimer," she said.

"No it's not, no it's not!" cried Mrs Jones, taking a loaf from the bread bin and absent-mindedly running the tap over it. "We said you could have a hamster when you were five, or a puppy or a kitten when you were six, and of course call it what you wish, oh my *stars*, look at that creature's toe-nails, if nails they can be called, but not a bird like that, a great hairy awful thing eating us out of house and home and as big as a fire extinguisher." But Arabel was looking at the raven and he was looking back at her. "His name's Mortimer," she said. And she put both arms round the raven, not an easy thing to do, all jammed in among the milk bottles as he was, and lifted him out.

"He's very heavy," she said, and set him down on the kitchen floor.

"So I should think, considering he's got a pound of sausages, a bowl of dripping, five pints of milk, half a pound of New Zealand cheddar, and a blackcurrant tart inside him," said Mrs Jones. "I'll open the window. Perhaps he'll fly out."

She opened the window. But Mortimer did not fly out. He was busy examining everything in the kitchen very thoroughly.

He tapped the table legs with his beak – they were metal, and clinked. Then he took everything out of the waste bin – a pound of peanut shells, two empty tins, and some jam tart cases. He particularly like the jam tart cases, which he pushed under the lino. Then he walked over to the fireplace – it was an old-fashioned kitchen – and began chipping out the mortar from between the bricks.

Mrs Jones had been gazing at the raven as if she were under a spell, but when he began on the fireplace, she said, "*Don't let him do that!*"

"Mortimer," said Arabel, "we'd like you not to do that, please."

Mortimer turned his head right round on its black feathery neck and gave Arabel a thoughtful, considering look. Then he made his first remark, which was a deep, hoarse, rasping croak.

"Kaarrk."

It said, as plainly as words: "Well, all right, I won't do it this time, but I make no promise that I won't do it *some* time. And I think you are being unreasonable."

"Wouldn't you like to see the rest of the house, Mortimer?" said Arabel. And she held open the kitchen door. Mortimer walked – he never hopped – very slowly through into the hall, and looked at the stairs. They seemed to interest him greatly. He began going up them hand over hand – or rather, beak over claw.

When he was halfway up, the telephone rang. It stood on the window-sill and Mortimer watched as Mrs Jones came to answer it.

Mr Jones was ringing from Colchester to ask if his wife wanted any oysters.

"Oysters!" she said. "That bird you left in the fridge has eaten sausages, cheese, dripping, blackcurrant tart, drunk five pints of milk, now he's chewing the stairs, and you ask if I want oysters? Perhaps I should feed him caviare as well?"

"Bird I left in the fridge?" Mr Jones was puzzled. "What bird, Martha?"

"That great black crow, or whatever it is. Arabel calls it Mortimer and she's leading it all over the house and now it's taken all the spools of cotton from my sewing drawer and is pushing them under the doormat."

"Not *it*, Ma. *He*. Mortimer," said Arabel, going to open the front door and take the letters from the postman. But Mortimer got there first, and received the letters in his beak.

The postman was so startled that he dropped his whole sack of mail in a puddle and gasped: "Nevermore will I stay later than half-past ten at the Oddfellows Ball or touch a drop stronger than Caribbean lemon, *nevermore!*"

"Nevermore," said Mortimer, pushing two bills and a post-card under the doormat. Then he retrieved the postcard again by spearing it clean through the middle. Mrs Jones let out a wail.

"Arabel, *will* you come in out of the street in your nightie! Look what that bird's done, chewing up the gas bill. Never-more, indeed! I should just about say it *was* nevermore. No I don't want any oysters, Ebenezer Jones."

Mr Jones couldn't understand all this, so he rang off. Five minutes later the telephone rang again. This time it was Mrs Jones's sister Brenda, to ask if Martha would like to play bingo

that evening. But this time Mortimer got to the phone first; he picked up the receiver with his claw, exactly as he had seen Mrs Jones do, delivered a loud clicking noise into it – *click* – and said: "Nevermore!"

Then he replaced the receiver.

"My goodness!" Brenda said to her husband. "Ben and Martha must have had a terrible quarrel; he answered the phone and he didn't sound a *bit* like himself!"

Meanwhile Mortimer had climbed upstairs and was in the bathroom trying the taps; it took him less than five minutes to work out how to turn them on. He liked to watch the cold water running, but the hot, with its clouds of steam, for some reason annoyed him, and he began throwing things at the hot tap: bits of soap, sponges, nail-brushes, face flannels.

They choked up the plug-hole and within a short time the water had overflowed and was flooding the bathroom.

"Mortimer, I think you'd better not stay in the bathroom," Arabel said.

Mortimer was good at giving black looks; he gave Arabel a black look. But she took no notice.

She had a red truck, which had once been filled with wooden building bricks. The bricks had been lost long ago, but the truck was in good repair.

"Mortimer, wouldn't you like a ride in this red truck?"

Mortimer thought he would. He climbed into the truck and stood there waiting. Arabel took hold of the handle and started pulling him along. When Mrs Jones noticed Arabel she nearly had a fit.

"It's not bad enough that you've adopted that big, ugly, sulky bird, but you have to pull him in a truck. Don't his legs work? Why can't he walk, may I ask?"

"He doesn't feel like walking just now," Arabel said.

"Of course! And I suppose he's *forgotten* how to *fly*?"

"I *like* pulling him on the truck," Arabel said, and she pulled him into the garden. Presently Mrs Jones went off to work at Round & Round, the gramophone shop, and Granny came in to look after Arabel. All Granny ever did was sit and knit. She liked answering the phone, too, but now every time it rang Mortimer got there first, picked up the receiver, and said: "Nevermore!"

People who rang up to order taxis were puzzled and said to one another, "Mr Jones must have retired."

They had baked beans for lunch. Mortimer enjoyed the baked beans, but his table-manners were very light-hearted. He liked knocking spoons and forks off the table, pushing them under the rush matting, and fetching them out again with a lot of excitement. Granny wasn't so keen on this.

While Granny was having her nap, Arabel looked at comics and Mortimer looked at the stairs. There seemed to be some-thing about stairs that appealed to him.

When Mr Jones came home at tea-time the first thing he said was: "What's happened to the three bottom steps?"

"What has, then?" asked Granny, who was short-sighted and anyway busy spreading jam.

"They aren't there."

"It wasn't Mortimer's fault," said Arabel. "He didn't know we need the stairs."

"Mortimer? Who's Mortimer?"

Just then Mrs Jones came home.

"That bird has got to go," said Mr Jones accusingly, the minute she had put down her shopping-basket and taken off her coat.

"Who's talking? *You* were the one who left him in the fridge."

Mortimer looked morose and sulky and black at Mr Jones's words. He sank his head between his shoulders and ruffled up the beard round his beak and turned his toes in as if he did not care one way or the other. But Arabel went so white that her father thought she was going to faint.

"If Mortimer goes," she said, "I shall cry *all* the time. Very likely I shall die!"

"Oh well . . ." said Mr Jones. "But, mind, if he stays, he's not to eat any more stairs!"

Just the same, during the next week or so, Mortimer did chew up six more stairs. The family had to go to bed by climbing an aluminium ladder.

There was a bit of trouble because he wanted to sleep in the fridge every night, but Mrs Jones put a stop to that; in the end he agreed to sleep in the airing-cupboard. Then there was a bit more trouble because he pushed all the soap and tooth-brushes under the bathroom lino and they couldn't get the door open. The fire-brigade had to climb through the window.

"He's not to be left alone in the house," Mr Jones said. "On the days when Arabel goes to play-group, Martha, he'll have to go to work with you."

"Why can't he come to play-group with me?" Arabel asked.

Mr Jones just laughed at that question.

Mrs Jones was not enthusiastic about taking Mortimer to work with her.

"So I'm to pull him up the High Street on that red truck? You must be joking."

"He can ride on your shopping-bag on wheels," Arabel said. "He'll like that."

At first the owners of the gramophone shop, Mr Round and Mr Toby Round, were quite pleased to have Mortimer sitting on the counter. People who lived in Rumbury Town heard about the raven in the record shop and were curious; they came in out of curiosity, and then they played records, and then, as often as not, bought the records. And at first Mortimer

was so astonished at the music that he sat still on the counter for hours at a time looking like a stuffed bird.

But presently Mortimer became bored by just sitting listening to music. He took to answering the telephone and saying, "Nevermore!" Then he began taking triangular bites out of the edges of records. After that it wasn't so easy to sell them. Then he noticed the spiral stairs which led down to the classic and folk departments. One morning Mr Round and Mr Toby Round and Mrs Jones were all very busy arranging a display of new issues in the shop window. When they had finished, they discovered that Mortimer had eaten the spiral staircase.

"Mrs Jones, you and your bird will have to go. We have kind, long-suffering natures, but Mortimer has done eight hundred and seventeen pounds, sixty-seven new pence' worth of damage. You may have a year to repay it. Please don't trouble to come in ever again."

"Glad I am *I* haven't such a kind, long-suffering nature," snapped Mrs Jones, and she dumped Mortimer on top of her wheeled shopping-bag and dragged him home.

"Stairs!" she said to Arabel. "What's the use of a bird who eats stairs? Gracious knows there's enough rubbish in the world – why can't he eat tonic bottles, or ice-cream cartons, or used cars, or oil slicks, tell me that? But no! he has to eat the only thing that joins the upstairs to the downstairs."

32

"Nevermore," said Mortimer.

"Tell that to the space cavalry!" said Mrs Jones.

Arabel and Mortimer went and sat side by side on the bottom rung of the fruit ladder, leaning against one another and very quiet.

"When I'm grown up," Arabel said to Mortimer, "we'll live in a house with a hundred stairs and you can eat them all."

Meanwhile, since the bank raid on the night Mr Jones had found Mortimer, several more places in Rumbury Town had been burgled. Brown's, the ironmongers, and Mr Finney the fishmonger, and the Tutti-Frutti Sweetie Shoppe.

On the day after Mrs Jones left Round & Round, she found another job, at Peter Stone, the jeweller's in the High Street. She had to take both Arabel and Mortimer with her to work, since play-group was finished till after Easter, and Granny had gone to Southend on a visit. Arabel pulled Mortimer to the shop every day on the red truck. Peter Stone had no objection to their coming.

"The more people in the shop, the less chance of a hold-up," he said. "Too much we're hearing about these Cash-and-Caret boys for my taste. Raided the supermarket yesterday, they did; took a thousand tins of Best Jamaica blend coffee, as the cashbox was jammed. Coffee! What would they want with a thousand tins?"

"Perhaps they were thirsty," Arabel said. She and Mortimer were looking at their reflections in a glass case full of bracelets. Mortimer tapped the glass in an experimental way with his beak.

"That bird, now," Peter Stone said, giving Mortimer a thoughtful look, "he'll behave himself? He won't go swallowing any diamonds? That brooch he's looking at now is worth forty thousand pounds."

Mrs Jones drew herself up. "Behave himself? Naturally he'll behave himself," she said. "Any diamonds he swallows I guarantee to replace!"

A police sergeant came into the shop. "I've a message for your husband," he said to Mrs Jones. "We've found a motorbike and we'd be glad if he'd step up to the station and say if he can identify it as the one that passed him the night the bank was robbed." Then he saw Mortimer. "Is that the bird that got knocked over? *He'd* better come along as well; we can see if he fits the dent in the petrol-tank."

"Nevermore," said Mortimer, who was eyeing a large clock under a glass dome.

"He'd better not talk like that to the Super," the sergeant said, "or he'll be charged with obstructing the police."

"Have you any theories about the identity of the gang?" Peter Stone asked.

"No, they always wear masks. But we're pretty sure they're locals and have a hideout somewhere in the district, because we always lose track of them so fast. One odd feature is that they have a very small accomplice, about the size of that bird there," the sergeant said, giving Mortimer a hard stare.

"How do you know?"

"When they robbed the supermarket, someone got in through the manager's cat-door and opened a window from inside. If birds had fingerprints," the sergeant said, "I wouldn't mind taking the dabs of that shifty-looking fowl. *He* could get through a cat-door easy enough."

34

"Your opinions are uncalled-for," said Mrs Jones. "Thoughtless our Mortimer may be, untidy at times, but honest as a Bath bun I'll have you know. And the night the supermarket was robbed he was in our airing-cupboard, with his head tucked under his wing."

"I've known some Bath buns not all they should be," said the sergeant.

Five minutes after the sergeant had gone, Peter Stone went off for his lunch.

And five minutes after *that*, two masked men walked into the shop.

One of them pointed a gun at Mrs Jones and Arabel, the other smashed a glass case and took out the diamond brooch which Peter Stone had said was worth forty thousand pounds.

Out of the gunman's pocket clambered a grey squirrel with an extremely villainous expression. It looked hopefully round the shop.

"Piece of apple-pie, this job," said the masked man who had taken the diamond brooch. "We'll give Sam the brooch and he can use the bird to hitch a ride to our pad. Then if the cops should stop us, they can't pin anything on us."

Mortimer, who was eating one of the cheese sandwiches

35

Mrs Jones had brought for her lunch, suddenly found a gun jammed against his ribs. The squirrel jumped on his back.

"You'd better co-operate, Coal-face," the gunman said. "This is a flyjack. Fly where Sam tells you, or you'll be blown to forty bits. Sam carries a bomb round his neck on a shoelace; all he has to do is pull out the pin with his teeth."

"Oh, please don't blow up Mortimer," Arabel said to the gunman. "I think he's forgotten how to fly."

"He'd better remember pretty fast."

"Oh dear, Mortimer, perhaps you'd better do what they say."

With a creak that could be heard all over the jeweller's shop, Mortimer unfolded his wings and, to his own surprise as much as anyone else's, flew out through the open door. The two thieves walked calmly after him.

As soon as they were gone, Mrs Jones went into hysterics, and Arabel rang the alarm buzzer.

In no time a police-van bounced to a stop outside, with siren screaming and lights flashing. Peter Stone came rushing back from the Fish Bar.

Mrs Jones was still having hysterics, but Arabel said: "Two masked gunmen stole a diamond brooch and gave it to a squirrel to carry away and he's flown off on our raven. Please get him back!"

"Where did the two men go?"

"They just walked off up the High Street."

"All sounds like a fishy tale to me," said the police sergeant – it was the same one who had been in earlier. "You sure you didn't just give the brooch to the bird and tell him to flit off with it to the nearest stolen-property dealer?"

"Oh, how could you say such a thing," wept Mrs Jones, "when our Mortimer's the best-hearted raven in Rumbury Town."

"Any clues?" said the sergeant to his men.

"There's a trail of cheese-crumbs here," said the constable. "We'll see how far we can follow them."

The police left, following the trail of cheese, which led all the way up Rumbury High Street, past the bank, past the fishmonger, past the supermarket, past the ironmonger, past the record shop, and stopped at the tube station.

"He's done us," said the sergeant. "Went on by tube. Did a large black bird buy a ticket to anywhere about ten minutes ago?" he asked Mr Gumbrell, the booking clerk.

"No."

"He could have got a ticket from a machine," one of the constables pointed out.

"They all say *Out of order.*"

"Anyway, why should a bird buy a ticket? He could just fly into a train," said another constable. "Maybe the girl's telling the truth."

All the passengers who had travelled on the Rumberloo Line that morning were asked if they had seen a large, black bird carrying a diamond brooch. None of them had.

"No offence, Mrs Jones," said Peter Stone, "but in these doubtful circumstances I'd just as soon you didn't come back after lunch. We'll say nothing about the forty thousand pounds for the brooch at present. Let's hope the bird is caught with it on him."

"He didn't take it," said Arabel. "You'll find out."

Arabel and Mrs Jones walked home to Number Six, Rainwater Crescent. Arabel was pale and silent, but Mrs Jones scolded all the way.

"Any bird with a scrap of gumption would have taken the brooch off that wretched little rat of a squirrel. Ashamed of himself, he ought to be! Nothing but trouble and aggravation we've had since Mortimer has been in the family; let's hope that's the last of him."

Arabel said she didn't want any tea, and went to bed, and cried herself to sleep.

That evening Mr Jones went up to the police station and identified the motorbike as the one that had passed him the night the bank had been robbed.

"Good," said the sergeant. "We found a couple of black feathers stuck to a bit of grease on the tank. If you ask *me*, that bird's up to his beak in all this murky business."

"How could he be?" Mr Jones said. "He was just crossing the road when the bike went by."

"Maybe they slipped him the cash as they passed."

"In that case we'd have seen it, wouldn't we? Do you know who the bike belongs to?"

"It was found abandoned on the Rumberloo Line embankment, where it comes out of the tunnel. We've a theory, but I'm not telling *you*; your family's under suspicion. Don't leave the district without informing us."

Mr Jones said he had no intention of leaving. "We want Mortimer found. My daughter's very upset."

Arabel was more than upset, she was in despair. She wandered about the house all day, looking at the things that reminded her of Mortimer – the fireplace bricks without any mortar, the plates with beak-sized chips missing, the chewed upholstery, all the articles that turned up under carpets and lino, and the missing stairs. The carpenter hadn't come yet to replace them, and Mr Jones was too dejected to nag him.

"I wouldn't have thought I'd get fond of a bird so quick," he said. "I miss his sulky face and his thoughtful ways and the sound of him crunching about the house. Eat up your tea, Arabel dearie, there's a good girl. I expect Mortimer will find his way home by and by."

But Arabel couldn't eat. Tears ran down her nose and on to her bread and jam until it was all soggy. That reminded her of the flood that Mortimer had caused by blocking up the bath plug, and the tears rolled even faster. "Mortimer doesn't know our address!" she said. "He doesn't even know our name!"

"We'll offer five pounds reward for his return," Mr Jones said.

"Five pounds!" cried Mrs Jones who had just come home from the supermarket where she now worked. "Five pounds you offer for the return of that Fiend when already we owe eight hundred and seventeen pounds and sixty-seven new pence to Round & Round, let alone the forty thousand to Peter Stone?"

Just the same Mr Jones stuck up his Reward sign in the sub-post-office, alongside one from Peter Stone, offering a thousand pounds for information that might lead to the return of his brooch, and similar ones from the bank, ironmonger and fishmonger.

Meanwhile, what of Mortimer and the squirrel?

They had flown as far as the tube station. There, Sam, by kicking Mortimer in the ribs and punching the top of his head, had directed him to fly into the station entrance.

Rumbury Town Station is very old. For nearly fifty years there had been only one slow, creaking old lift to take people down to the trains. People too impatient to wait for it had to walk down about a thousand spiral stairs. But lately the station had been modernized by the addition of a handsome pair of escalators which replaced the spiral stairs. Nothing else was modern.

Not so many trains stop at Rumbury Town; most of them rush straight through from Nutmeg Hill to Canon's Green.

Old Mr Gumbrell, the booking clerk, was Mr Jones's uncle. Besides selling tickets, he also ran the lift, and when he had sold twelve tickets he would lock up his office and take the lift down. This meant that sometimes people had to wait a very long time for a lift, but it didn't much matter as there probably wouldn't be a train for hours. However, in the end there were complaints, which was why the escalators were installed. Mr Gumbrell enjoyed riding on these, which he called escatailors; he used to leave the lift at the bottom and travel back up the moving stairs.

He did this on the day when Mortimer and the squirrel arrived. He ran the lift slowly down, never noticing that Mortimer, with Sam the squirrel still grimly clutching him, was perched high up near the ceiling on the frame of a poster.

Mr Gumbrell left the lift at the bottom, and sailed back up the escalator, mumbling to himself: "Arr, these-ere moving stairs do be an amazing wonder of science. What ever will they think of next?"

When Mr Gumbrell got to the top again he found the police there, examining the trail of cheese-crumbs which stopped outside the station entrance. They stayed a long time, but Mr Gumbrell could give them no useful information.

The phone rang. It was Mr Jones.

"Is that you, Uncle Arthur?"

"O' course it's me! Who else would it be?"

"We just wondered if you'd seen Arabel's raven. The trail of cheese-crumbs led up your way, the police said."

"No, I have not seen a raven," snapped Mr Gumbrell. "Coppers a-bothering here all afternoon, but still I haven't! Nor I haven't seen a Socrates bird nor a cassodactyl nor a pterowary. This is a tube station, not a zoological garden."

"Will you keep a look-out, just the same?" said Mr Jones.

Mr Gumbrell thumped back the receiver. He was fed up at all the bother. "If I wait here any longer," he said, "likely the militia and the beef-guards and the horse-eaters and the traffic wardens'll be along too. I'm closing up."

Rumbury Town Station was not supposed to be closed except between 1 a.m. and 5 a.m., but in fact Mr Gumbrell often did close it earlier if his bad toe was bothering him. No one had complained yet.

"Even if me toe ain't aching now, likely it'll start any minute with all this willocking about," Mr Gumbrell argued to himself. So he switched off the escalators, locked the lift gates and ticket office, turned out the lights, rang up Nutmeg Hill and Canon's Green to tell them not to let any trains stop, padlocked the big main mesh gates, and stomped off home to supper.

Next morning there were several people waiting to catch the first train to work when Mr Gumbrell arrived to open up. They bustled in as soon as he slid the gates back and didn't stop at the booking-office for they all had season tickets. But when they reached the top of the escalator they did stop, in dismay and astonishment.

For the escalators were not there: nothing but a big, gaping, black hole.

"Someone's pinched the stairs," said a Covent Garden porter.

"Don't be so soft. How could you pinch an escalator?" said a milkman.

"Well, they're gone, aren't they?" said a bus conductor. "What's *your* theory? Earthquake? Sunk into the ground?"

Mr Gumbrell stood scratching his head. "Took my escatailors," he said sorrowfully. "What did they want to go and

41

do that for? If they'd 'a took the lift, now, I wouldn't 'a minded near as much. Well, all you lot'll have to go down in the lift." But when he pulled the lever that ought to have brought the lift up, nothing happened.

"And I'll tell you why," said the train driver, peering through the closed top gates. "Someone's been and chawed through the lift cable."

"Sawed through it?"

"No, kind of chewed or haggled through; a right messy job. Lucky the current was switched off, or whoever done it would have been frizzled like popcorn."

"Someone's been sabotaging the station," said the bus conductor. "Football fans, is my guess."

"Someone ought to tell the cops." ·

"Cops!" grumbled Mr Gumbrell. "Not likely! Had enough of them in yesterday a-scavenging about for ravens and squirrels."

Another reason why he did not want the police called in was because he didn't want to admit that he had left the station unattended for so long. But the early travellers, finding they could not get a train there, walked off to the next stop down the line, Nutmeg Hill. They told their friends at work what had happened, and the story spread. Presently a reporter from the *Rumbury Borough News* rang up the tube station for confirmation of the tale.

"Is that Rumbury Town Station? Can you tell me, please, if the trains are running normally?"

"Nevermore!" croaked a harsh voice, and the receiver was thumped down.

"You'd better go up there and have a look round," said the editor, when his reporter told him of this puzzling conversation.

So the reporter – his name was Dick Otter – took a bus up to the tube station. Old Mr Gumbrell with his white whiskers, seated inside the ticket kiosk, was like some wizened goblin with his little piles of magic cards telling people where they could go.

"Is the station open?" Dick asked.

"*You* walked in, didn't you? But you can't *go* anywhere," said Mr Gumbrell.

Dick went over and looked at the gaping hole where the moving staircase used to be. Mr Gumbrell had hung a couple of chains across, to stop people falling down.

Then Dick peered through the lift gates, and down the shaft.

"Who do you think took the escalators?" he asked, getting out his notebook.

Mr Gumbrell had been thinking about this a good deal, on and off, during the morning. "Spooks," he replied. "Spooks what doesn't like modern inventions. I reckon the station's haunted. As I've bin sitting here this morning, there's a ghostly voice that sometimes comes and croaks in me lughole. 'Nevermore,' it says, 'nevermore.' That's one reason why I haven't informed the cops. What could they do? What that voice means is that this station shall nevermore be used."

"I see," said Dick thoughtfully. In his notebook he wrote: *Is Tube Station Haunted or is Booking Clerk Round the Bend?*

"What else makes you think it's haunted?" he asked.

"Well," said Mr Gumbrell, "there couldn't *be* anybody downstairs, could there? I locked up last night, when the nine o'clock south had gone, and I phoned 'em at Nutmeg Hill and Canon's Green not to let any trains stop here till I give 'em word again. No one would've gone down this end after that, and yet sometimes I thinks as I can hear voices down the lift shaft a-calling out '*help, help*'! Which is a contradiction of nature, since, like I said, no one could be down there."

"Supposing they'd gone down last night before you locked up?"

"Then they'd 'a caught the nine o'clock south, wouldn't they? No, 'tis ghosties down there all right."

"You think you can hear voices crying 'help, help', down the lift shaft?" Dick went and listened but there was nothing to be heard at that moment.

"Likely I'm the only man as can hear 'em," said Mr Gumbrell.

"It seems to me I can *smell* something though," Dick said, sniffing.

Up from the lift shaft floated the usual smell of tube station – a queer, warm, dusty metallic smell like powdered ginger. But as well as that there was another smell – fragrant and tantalizing. "Smells to me like coffee," Dick said. "Well, I'd like to get some pictures of the station." He went over to the public call-box and dialled his office, to get a photographer. But as he waited with the coin in his hand, ready to put it in the slot when the pips went, something large and black suddenly wafted past his head in the gloom, snatched the receiver from him, and whispered harshly in his ear: "Nevermore!"

Next day the *Rumbury Borough News* had a headline: IS OUR TUBE STATION HAUNTED? And beneath: "Mr Gumbrell, ticket collector and booking clerk there for the last forty years, asserts that it is. 'Ghosts sit downstairs drinking coffee,' he says."

"Shan't be able to meet people's eyes in the street," said Mr Jones at breakfast. "Going barmy Uncle Arthur is, without a doubt. Haunted tube station? Take him along to see the doctor, shall I?"

The postman rang, with a letter on Recorded Delivery from a firm of lawyers: Messrs Gumme, Harbottle, Inkpen and Rule. It said:

> *Dear Madam,*
> *Acting as solicitors for Mr Round and Mr Toby Round, we wish to know when it will be convenient for you to pay the eight hundred and seventeen pounds and sixty-seven new pence' worth of damage that you owe our clients for Destruction of Premises?*

This threw Mrs Jones into a dreadful flutter. "That I should live to see the day when we are turned out of house and home on account of a fiend of a bird fetched in off the street by my own husband."

44

"Well, you haven't lived to see the day yet," said Mr Jones. "Wild creatures, ravens are counted as, in law, so we can't be held responsible for the bird's actions. I'll go round and tell them so, and *you'd* better do something to cheer up Arabel. I've never seen the child so thin and mopey."

He drove his taxi up to Round & Round, the record shop, but, strangely enough, neither Mr Round nor Mr Toby Round was to be seen; the place was locked, silent, and dusty.

After trying to persuade Arabel to eat her breakfast – which was no use, as Arabel wouldn't touch it – Mrs Jones decided to ring Uncle Arthur and tell him he should see a doctor for his nerves. She called up the tube station, but the telephone rang and nobody answered. (In fact the reason for this was that a great many sightseers, having read the piece in the newspaper, had come to stare at the station, and Mr Gumbrell was having a fine time telling them all about the ghosties. While Mrs Jones was still holding the telephone and listening, the front-door bell rang.

"Trouble, trouble, nothing but trouble," grumbled Mrs Jones. "Here, Arabel lovey, hold the phone and say 'Hello, Uncle Arthur, Mum wants to speak to you' if he answers, will you, while I see who's at the front door."

45

Arabel took the receiver and Mrs Jones went to the front door, where there were two policemen. She let out a screech.

"It's no use that pair of sharks sending you to arrest me for their eight hundred and seventeen pounds – I haven't got it if you were turn me upside-down and shake me till September!"

The police looked puzzled and one of them said, "I reckon there's some mistake? We don't want to turn you upside-down – we came to ask you if you recognize this?"

He held out a small object in the palm of his hand.

Mrs Jones had a close look at it.

"Why certainly I do," she said. "That's Mr Round's tie-pin – the one he had made from one of his back teeth when it fell out as he ate a plateful of Irish stew."

Meanwhile Arabel was still sitting on the half-finished new stairs holding the phone to her ear, when all at once she heard a hoarse whisper:

"Nevermore!"

Arabel was so astonished she almost dropped the telephone. She looked all round her – nobody there. Then she looked back at the phone, but it had gone silent again. After a minute a different voice barked: "Who's that?"

"Hello, Uncle Arthur, it's me, Arabel, Mum wants to speak to you."

"Well, I don't want to speak to her," said Mr Gumbrell, and he hung up.

Arabel sat on the stairs and said to herself: "That was Mortimer. He must be up at the tube station because that's where Uncle Arthur is."

Arabel had often travelled by tube, and knew the way to the station. She got her red truck, and put on her thick, warm, woolly coat, and she went out of the back door because her mother was still talking at the front and Arabel didn't want to be stopped. She walked up the High Street, past the bank. The manager looked out and said to himself: "That child's too young to be out on her own, I'd better follow her and find who she belongs to."

He started after her.

Next Arabel passed the supermarket. The manager looked out and said to himself: "That's Mrs Jones's little girl. I'll just nip after her and ask her where her mother's got to today." So he followed Arabel.

Then she passed the Round & Round record shop, but there was nobody in it, and Mr Jones had become tired of waiting and driven off in his taxi.

Then she passed Peter Stone, the jeweller. Peter Stone saw her through the window and thought: "That girl looks as if she knows where she means to go. And she was the only one who showed any sense after my burglary. Maybe it was a true story about the squirrel and the raven. Anyway, no harm following her to see where she goes." So he locked up his shop and followed.

Arabel passed the fire-station. Usually the firemen waved to her – they had been friendly ever since they had had to come and climb in the Joneses' bathroom window – but today they were all hastily pulling on their helmets and rushing about. And just as she had gone past, the fire-engine shot out and by her, going lickety-spit.

Presently Arabel came to the tube station. The first person she saw there was her great-aunt Annie Gumbrell.

"*Arabel Jones!* What are you doing walking up the High Street by yourself, liable to get run over and kidnapped and murdered. The idea! Where's your mother? And where are you going?"

"I'm looking for Mortimer," said Arabel, and she kept on going. "I've stayed on the same side all the way; I didn't have to cross over," she said over her shoulder as she went into the tube station.

Aunt Annie had come up to the station to tell Uncle Arthur that he was behaving foolishly and had better come home, but she couldn't get near him because of the crowd. In fact Arabel was the only person who *could* get into the station entrance now, because she was so small. When Arabel was inside somebody kindly picked her up and set her on top of a ticket machine so that she could see.

"What's happening?" she asked.

47

"They reckon someone's stuck in the lift, down at the bottom. So they're a-going to send down a fireman, and he'll go in through the trap-door in the roof of the lift and fetch 'em back," said her great-uncle Arthur, who happened to be standing by her. "I've told 'em and told 'em 'tis ghosties, but they don't take no notice."

Now the firemen, who had been taking a careful look at the lift, asked everybody to please step out into the street to make room. Then they rigged up a light, because the station was so dark, and they brought in a hoist, which was mostly used for rescuing people who got stuck up church spires or on the roofs of burning buildings. They let down a fireman in a sling, and the whole population of Rumbury Town, by now standing in the street outside, said: "Coo!" and held its breath.

Presently a shout came from below.

"They've found someone," said the firemen, and everybody said "Coo!" again and held their breath some more.

Just at this moment Arabel (still sitting on top of the ticket machine for she was in no one's way there) felt a thump on her right shoulder. It was lucky that she had put on her thick warm woolly coat, for two claws took hold of her shoulder

with a grip like a bulldog clip. A loving croak in her ear said: "Nevermore!"

"Mortimer!" said Arabel, and she was so pleased that she might have toppled off the ticket machine if Mortimer hadn't spread out his wings like a tightrope-walker's umbrella and balanced them both.

Mortimer was just as pleased to see Arabel as she was to see him. When he had them both balanced he wrapped his left-hand wing round her and said "Nevermore" five or six times over, in tones of great satisfaction and enthusiasm.

"Look, Mortimer, they're bringing someone up."

Slowly, slowly, up came the sling, and who should climb out but Mr Toby Round, looking hungry and sorry for himself. The minute he was landed all sorts of helpful people, St John ambulance men and stretcher-bearers and clergymen and the matron of the Rumbury Central Hospital, all rushed at him with bandages and cups of tea and said, "Are you all right?"

They would have taken him away, but he said he wanted to wait for his brother.

The sling went down again at once. In a few minutes up it came with the other Mr Round. As soon as he landed he noticed Arabel and Mortimer perched on the ticket machine, and the sight of them seemed to set him in a passion.

"Grab that bird!" he shouted. "*He's* the cause of all the trouble! Gnawed through the lift cable and ate the escalator and had my brother and me trapped in utter discomfort for forty-eight hours!"

"And what was you a-doing down there," said Gumbrell suspiciously, "after the nine o'clock south had come and gone?"

Just at this moment a whole van-load of police arrived with Mrs Jones, who seemed half distracted.

"*There* you are!" she screamed when she saw Arabel. "And me nearly frantic, *oh*, my goodness, there's that great awful bird, as if we hadn't enough to worry us!"

But the police swarmed about the Round brothers, and the sergeant said, "I have a warrant to arrest you two on suspicion of having pinched the cash from the bank last month and if you want to know why we think it's you that did it, it's because we found your tooth tie-pin left behind in the safe and one of Toby's fingerprints on the abandoned motorbike. And I shouldn't wonder if you did the jobs at the supermarket and the jeweller's and all the others too!"

"It's not true!" shouted Mr Toby Round. "We didn't do it! We didn't do *any* of them. We were staying with my sister-in-law at Romford on each occasion. Her name's Mrs Flossie Wilkes and she lives at Two-nought-nought-one Station Approach. If you ask *my* opinion that raven is the thief——"

But the sergeant had pulled Mr Toby Round's hand from his pocket to put a handcuff on it, and, when he did so, what should come out as well but Sam the squirrel, and what should Sam be clutching in his paws but Mr Peter Stone's diamond brooch.

So everybody said "Coo!" again. And Mr Round and Mr Toby Round were taken off to Rumbury Hill police station. The police sergeant hitched a ride in the firemen's sling and went down the lift shaft and had a look round. He found the money that had been stolen from the bank, all packed in the plastic dustbins that had been stolen from Brown's the iron-mongers, and he found nine hundred and ninety-nine of the thousand tins of Best Jamaica blend coffee stolen from the supermarket, and a whole lot of other things that must have been stolen from different premises all over Rumbury Town.

While he was making these exciting discoveries down below, up above Mrs Jones was saying: "Arabel, you come home directly, and don't you dare go out on your own ever again!"

"Nevermore!" said Mortimer.

So Arabel climbed down from the ticket machine, with Mortimer still on her shoulder.

"Here!" said Uncle Arthur, who had been silent for a long time, turning things over in his mind, "that bird ought to be arrested too, if he's the one what ate my escatailors and put my lift out of order! How do we know he wasn't in with those blokes and their burglaries? He was the one what helped the squirrel make off with the di'mond brooch."

"He was flyjacked; he couldn't help it," said Arabel.

"Far from being arrested," said the bank manager, "he'll get a reward from the bank for helping to bring the criminals to justice."

"And he'll get one from me too," said Peter Stone.

"And from me," said the supermarket manager.

"Come along Arabel, do," said Mrs Jones, "oh my gracious, look at the time, your father'll be home wanting his tea and wondering where in the world we've got to!"

Arabel collected her red truck, which she had left outside, and Mortimer climbed on to it.

"My stars!" cried Mrs Jones. "You're not going to pull that great sulky bird all the way home on the truck when we know perfectly *well* he can fly, the lazy thing? Never did I hear anything so outrageous, never!"

"He likes being pulled," said Arabel, so that was the way they went home. The bank manager and the supermarket manager and Mr Peter Stone and quite a lot of other people saw them as far as the gate.

Mr Jones was inside and had just made a pot of tea. When he saw them come in the front gate he poured out an egg-cupful for Mortimer.

They all sat round the kitchen table and had tea. Mortimer had several egg-cupfuls, and as for Arabel, she made up for all the meals she had missed while Mortimer had been lost.

ZLATEH THE GOAT

Isaac Bashevis Singer

At Hanukkah time the road from the village to the town is usually covered with snow, but this year the winter had been a mild one. Hanukkah had almost come, yet little snow had fallen. The sun shone most of the time. The peasants complained that because of the dry weather there would be a poor harvest of winter grain. New grass sprouted, and the peasants sent their cattle out to pasture.

For Reuven the furrier it was a bad year, and after long hesitation he decided to sell Zlateh the goat. She was old and gave little milk. Feyvel the town butcher had offered eight gulden for her. Such a sum would buy Hanukkah candles, potatoes and oil for pancakes, gifts for the children, and other holiday necessaries for the house. Reuven told his oldest boy Aaron to take the goat to town.

Aaron understood what taking the goat to Feyvel meant, but he had to obey his fasther. Leah, his mother, wiped the tears from her eyes when she heard the news. Aaron's younger sisters, Anna and Miriam, cried loudly. Aaron put on his quilted jacket and a cap with earmuffs, bound a rope around Zlateh's neck, and took along two slices of bread with cheese to eat on the road. Aaron was supposed to deliver the goat by evening, spend the night at the butcher's, and return the next day with the money.

While the family said good-bye to the goat, and Aaron

53

placed the rope around her neck, Zlateh stood as patiently and good-naturedly as ever. She licked Reuven's hand. She shook her small white beard. Zlateh trusted human beings. She knew that they always fed her and never did her any harm.

When Aaron brought her out on the road to town, she seemed somewhat astonished. She'd never been led in that direction before. She looked back at him questioningly, as if to say, "Where are you taking me?" But after a while she seemed to come to the conclusion that a goat shouldn't ask questions. Still, the road was different. They passed new fields, pastures, and huts with thatched roofs. Here and there a dog barked and came running after them, but Aaron chased it away with his stick.

The sun was shining when Aaron left the village. Suddenly the weather changed. A large black cloud with a bluish centre appeared in the east and spread itself rapidly over the sky. A cold wind blew in with it. The crows flew low, croaking. At first it looked as if it would rain, but instead it began to hail as in summer. It was early in the day, but it became dark as dusk. After a while the hail turned to snow.

In his twelve years Aaron had seen all kinds of weather, but he had never experienced a snow like this one. It was so dense it shut out the light of the day. In a short time their path was completely covered. The wind became as cold as ice. The road to town was narrow and winding. Aaron no longer knew where he was. He could not see through the snow. The cold soon penetrated his quilted jacket.

At first Zlateh didn't seem to mind the change in weather. She too was twelve years old and knew what winter meant. But when her legs sank deeper and deeper into the snow, she began to turn her head and look at Aaron in wonderment. Her mild eyes seemed to ask, "Why are we out in such a storm?" Aaron hoped that a peasant would come along with his cart, but no one passed by.

.The snow grew thicker, falling to the ground in large, whirling flakes. Beneath it Aaron's boots touched the softness of a ploughed field. He realized that he was no longer on the road. He had gone astray. He could no longer make out which was east or west, which way was the village, the town. The wind whistled, howled, whirled the snow about in eddies. It looked as if white imps were playing tag on the fields. A white dust rose above the ground. Zlateh stopped. She could walk no longer. Stubbornly she anchored her cleft hooves in the earth and bleated as if pleading to be taken home. Icicles hung from her white beard, and her horns were glazed with frost.

Aaron did not want to admit the danger, but he knew just the same that if they did not find shelter they would freeze to death. This was no ordinary storm. It was a mighty blizzard. The snowfall had reached his knees. His hands were numb, and he could no longer feel his toes. He choked when he breathed. His nose felt like wood, and he rubbed it with snow. Zlateh's bleating began to sound like crying. Those humans in whom she had so much confidence had dragged her into a trap. Aaron began to pray to God for himself and for the innocent animal.

Suddenly he made out the shape of a hill. He wondered what it could be. Who had piled snow into such a huge heap? He moved towards it, dragging Zlateh after him. When he came near it, he realized that it was a large haystack which the snow had blanketed.

Aaron saw immediately that they were saved. With great effort he dug his way through the snow. He was a village boy and knew what to do. When he reached the hay, he hollowed out a nest for himself and the goat. No matter how cold it may be outside, in the hay it is always warm. And hay was food for Zlateh. The moment she smelled it she became contented and began to eat. Outside the snow continued to fall. It quickly covered the passageway Aaron had dug. But a boy and an animal need to breathe, and there was hardly any air in their hideout. Aaron bored a kind of window through the hay and snow and carefully kept the passage clear.

Zlateh, having eaten her fill, sat down on her hind legs and seemed to have regained her confidence in man. Aaron ate his two slices of bread and cheese, but after the difficult journey he was still hungry. He looked at Zlateh and noticed her udders were full. He lay down next to her, placing himself so that when he milked her he could squirt the milk into his mouth. It was rich and sweet. Zlateh was not accustomed to being milked that way, but she did not resist. On the contrary, she seemed eager to reward Aaron for bringing her to a shelter whose very walls, floor, and ceiling were made of food.

Through the window Aaron could catch a glimpse of the chaos outside. The wind carried before it whole drifts of snow. It was completely dark, and he did not know whether night had already come or whether it was the darkness of the storm. Thank God that in the hay it was not cold. The dried grass and field flowers exuded the warmth of the summer sun. Zlateh ate frequently; she nibbled from above, below, from the left and right. Her body gave forth an animal warmth, and Aaron cuddled up to her. He had always loved Zlateh, but now she was like a sister. He was alone, cut off from his family, and wanted to talk. He began to talk to Zlateh. "Zlateh, what do you think about what has happened to us?" he asked.

"Maaaa," Zlateh answered.

"If we hadn't found this stack of hay, we would both be frozen stiff by now," Aaron said.

"Maaaa," was the goat's reply.

"If the snow keeps on falling like this, we may have to stay here for days," Aaron explained.

"Maaaa," Zlateh bleated.

"What does 'Maaaa' mean?" Aaron asked. "You'd better speak up clearly."

"Maaaa. Maaaa," Zlateh tried.

"Well, let it be 'Maaaa' then," Aaron said patiently. "You can't speak, but I know you understand. I need you and you need me. Isn't that right?"

"Maaaa."

Aaron became sleepy. He made a pillow out of some hay, leaned his head on it, and dozed off. Zlateh too fell asleep.

When Aaron opened his eyes, he didn't know whether it

was morning or night. The snow had blocked up his window. He tried to clear it, but when he had bored through to the length of his arm, he still hadn't reached the outside. Luckily he had his stick with him and was able to break through to the open air. It was still dark outside. The snow continued to fall and the wind wailed, first with one voice and then with many. Sometimes it had the sound of devilish laughter. Zlateh too awoke, and when Aaron greeted her, she answered, "Maaaa." Yes, Zlateh's language consisted of only one word, but it meant many things. Now she was saying, "We must accept all that God gives us – heat, cold, hunger, satisfaction, light, and darkness."

Aaron had awakened hungry. He had eaten up his food, but Zlateh had plenty of milk.

For three days Aaron and Zlateh stayed in the haystack. Aaron had always loved Zlateh, but in these three days he loved her more and more. She fed him with her milk and helped him keep warm. She comforted him with her patience. He told her many stories, and she always cocked her ears and listened. When he patted her, she licked his hand and his face. Then she said, "Maaaa," and he knew it meant, I love you too.

The snow fell for three days, though after the first day it was not as thick and the wind quieted down. Sometimes Aaron felt that there could never have been a summer, that the snow had always fallen, ever since he could remember. He, Aaron, never had a father or mother or sisters. He was a snow child, born of the snow, and so was Zlateh. It was so quiet in the hay that his ears rang in the stillness. Aaron and Zlateh slept all night and a good part of the day. As for Aaron's dreams, they were all about warm weather. He dreamed of green fields, trees covered with blossoms, clear brooks, and singing birds. By the third night the snow had stopped, but Aaron did not dare to find his way home in the darkness. The sky became clear and the moon shone, casting silvery nets on the snow. Aaron dug his way out and looked at the world. It was all white, quiet, dreaming dreams of heavenly splendour. The stars were large and close. The moon swam in the sky as in a sea.

On the morning of the fourth day Aaron heard the ringing of sleigh bells. The haystack was not far from the road. The peasant who drove the sleigh pointed out the way to him – not to the town and Feyvel the butcher, but home to the village. Aaron had decided in the haystack that he would never part with Zlateh.

Aaron's family and their neighbours had searched for the boy and the goat but had found no trace of them during the storm. They feared they were lost. Aaron's mother and sisters cried for him; his father remained silent and gloomy. Suddenly one of the neighbours came running to their house with the news that Aaron and Zlateh were coming up the road.

There was great joy in the family. Aaron told them how he had found the stack of hay and how Zlateh had fed him with her milk. Aaron's sisters kissed and hugged Zlateh and gave her a special treat of chopped carrots and potato peel, which Zlateh gobbled up hungrily.

Nobody ever again thought of selling Zlateh, and now that the cold weather had finally set in, the villagers needed the services of Reuven the furrier once more. When Hanukkah came, Aaron's mother was able to fry pancakes every evening, and Zlateh got her portion too. Even though Zlateh had her own pen, she often came to the kitchen, knocking on the door with her horns to indicate that she was ready to visit, and she was always admitted. In the evening Aaron, Miriam, and Anna played dreidel. Zlateh sat near the stove watching the children and the flickering of the Hanukkah candles.

Once in a while Aaron would ask her, "Zlateh, do you remember the three days we spent together?"

And Zlateh would scratch her neck with a horn, shake her white bearded head and come out with the single sound which expressed all her thoughts, and all her love.

THE CHRISTMAS PONY

Lincoln Steffens

What interested me in our new neighbourhood was not the school, nor the room I was to have in the new house all to myself, but the stable which was built back of the house. My father let me direct the making of a stall, a little smaller than the other stalls, for my pony, and I prayed and hoped and my sister Lou believed that that meant that I would get the pony, perhaps for Christmas. I pointed out to her that there were three other stalls and no horses at all. This I said in order that she should answer it. She could not. My father, sounded out, said that some day we might have horses and a cow; meanwhile a stable added to the value of a house. "Some day" is a pain to a boy who lives in and knows only "now". My good little sisters, to comfort me, remarked that Christmas was coming, but Christmas was always coming and grown-ups were always talking about it, asking you what you wanted and then giving you what they wanted you to have.

Though everybody knew what I wanted, I told them all again. My mother knew that I told God, too, every night. I wanted a pony, and to make sure they understood, I declared that I wanted nothing else.

"Nothing but a pony?" my father asked.

"Nothing," I said.

"Not even a pair of high boots?"

That was hard. I did want boots, but I stuck to the pony. "No, not even boots."

59

"Nor candy? There ought to be something to fill your stocking with, and Santa Claus can't put a pony into a stocking."

That was true, and he couldn't lead a pony down the chimney either. But no. "All I want is a pony," I said. "If I can't have a pony, give me nothing, nothing."

Now I had been looking myself for the pony I wanted, going to sales stables, inquiring of horsemen, and I had seen several that would do. My father let me "try" them. I tried so many ponies that I was learning fast to sit a horse. I chose several, but my father always found some fault with them. I was in despair. When Christmas was at hand I had given up all hope of a pony, and on Christmas Eve I hung up my stocking along with my sisters', of whom, by the way, I now had three.

I haven't mentioned my sisters or their coming because, you understand, they were girls, and girls, young girls, counted for nothing in my manly life. They did not mind me either; they were so happy that Christmas Eve that I caught some of their merriment. I speculated on what I'd get. I hung up the biggest stocking I had, and we all went reluctantly to bed to wait until morning. Not to sleep; not right away. We were told that we must not only sleep promptly, we must not wake up until seven-thirty – if we did, we must not go to the fireplace for our Christmas. Impossible.

We did sleep that night, but we woke up at six a.m. We lay in our beds and debated through the open doors whether to obey until, say, half-past six. Then we bolted. I don't know who started it, but there was a rush. We all disobeyed; we raced to disobey and get first to the fireplace in the front room downstairs. And there they were, the gifts, all sorts of wonderful things, mixed-up piles of presents; only, as I disentangled the mess, I saw that my stocking was empty; it hung limp; not a thing in it; and under and around it – nothing. My sisters had knelt down, each by her pile of gifts; they were squealing with delight, until they looked up and saw me standing there in my nightgown with nothing. They left their piles to come to me and look with me at my empty place. Nothing. They felt my stocking: nothing.

I don't remember whether I cried at that moment, but my sisters did. They ran with me back to my bed, and there we all cried until I became indignant. That helped some. I got up, dressed, and driving my sisters away, I went alone out into the yard, down to the stable, and there, all by myself, I wept. My mother came out to me by and by; she found me in my pony stall, sobbing on the floor, and she tried to comfort me. But I heard my father outside; he had come part way with her, and she was having some sort of angry quarrel with him. She tried to comfort me; besought me to come to breakfast. I could not; I wanted no comfort and no breakfast. She left me and went on into the house with sharp words for my father.

I don't know what kind of breakfast the family had. My sisters said it was "awful". They were ashamed to enjoy their own toys. They came to me, and I was rude. I ran away from

61

them. I went around to the front of the house, sat down on the steps, and, the crying over, I ached. I was wronged, I was hurt – I can feel now what I felt then, and I am sure that if one could see the wounds upon our hearts, there would be found still upon mine a scar from that terrible Christmas morning. And my father, the practical joker, he must have been hurt, too, a little. I saw him looking out of the window. He was watching me or something for an hour or two, drawing back the curtain ever so little lest I catch him, but I saw his face, and I think I can see now the anxiety upon it, the worried impatience.

After, I don't know how long, surely an hour or two, I was brought to the climax of my agony by the sight of a man riding a pony down the street, a pony and a brand-new saddle; the most beautiful saddle I ever saw, and it was a boy's saddle; the man's feet were not in the stirrups; his legs were too long. The outfit was perfect; it was the realization of all my dreams, the answer to all my prayers. A fine new bridle, with a light curb bit. And the pony! As he drew near, I saw that the pony was really a small horse – what we called an Indian pony, a bay, with black mane and tail, and one white foot and a white star on his forehead. For such a horse as that I would have given, I could have given, anything.

But the man, a dishevelled fellow with a blackened eye and a fresh-cut face, came along, reading the numbers on the houses, and, as my hopes – my impossible hopes – rose, he looked at our door and passed by, he and the pony, and the saddle and the bridle. Too much. I fell upon the steps, and having wept before, I broke now into such a flood of tears that I was a floating wreck when I heard a voice.

"Say, kid," it said, "do you know a boy named Lennie Steffens?"

I looked up. It was the man on the pony, back again, at our horse block.

"Yes," I spluttered through my tears, "That's me."

"Well," he said, "then this is your horse. I've been looking all over for you and your house. Why don't you put your number where it can be seen?"

"Get down," I said, running out to him.

He went on saying something about "ought to have got here at seven o'clock; told me to bring the nag here and tie him to your post and leave him for you. But I got into a drunk – and a fight – and a hospital – and –"

"Get down," I said.

He got down, and he boosted me up to the saddle. He offered to fit the stirrups to me, but I didn't want him to. I wanted to ride.

"What's the matter with you?" he said, angrily. "What you crying for? Don't you like the horse? He's a dandy, this horse. I know him of old. He's fine at cattle; he'll drive 'em alone."

I hardly heard, I could scarcely wait, but he persisted. He adjusted the stirrups, and then, finally, off I rode, slowly, at a walk, so happy, so thrilled, that I did not know what I was doing. I did not look back at the house or the man, I rode off up the street, taking note of everything – of the reins, of the pony's long mane, of the carved leather saddle. I had never known anything so beautiful. And mine! I was going to ride up past Miss Kay's house. But I noticed on the horn of the saddle some stains like rain-drops, so I turned and trotted home, not to the house but to the stable. There was the

family, father, mother, sisters, all working for me, all happy.
They had been putting in place the tools of my new business:
blankets, currycomb, brush, pitchfork – everything, and there
was hay in the loft.

"What did you come back so soon for?" somebody asked.
"Why didn't you go on riding?"

I pointed to the stains. "I wasn't going to get my new saddle
rained on," I said. And my father laughed. "It isn't raining,"
he said. "Those are not rain-drops."

"They are tears," my mother gasped, and she gave my
father a look which sent him off to the house. Worse still, my
mother offered to wipe away the tears still running out of my
eyes. I gave her such a look as she had given him, and she
went off after my father, drying her own tears. My sisters
remained and we all unsaddled the pony, put on his halter,
led him to his stall, tied and fed him. It began really to rain; so
all the rest of that memorable day we curried and combed that
pony. The girls plaited his mane, forelock, and tail, while I
pitchforked hay to him and curried and brushed, curried and
brushed. For a change we brought him out to drink; we led

him up and down, blanketed like a race-horse; we took turns at that. But the best, the most inexhaustible fun, was to clean him. When we went reluctantly to our midday Christmas dinner, we all smelt of horse, and my sisters had to wash their faces and hands. I was asked to, but I wouldn't until my mother bade me look in the mirror. Then I washed up – quick. My face was caked with the muddy lines of tears that had coursed over my cheeks to my mouth. Having washed away that shame, I ate my dinner, and as I ate I grew hungrier and hungrier. It was my first meal that day, and as I filled up on the turkey and the stuffing, the cranberries and the pies, the fruit and the nuts – as I swelled, I could laugh. My mother said I still choked and sobbed now and then, but I laughed, too; I saw and enjoyed my sisters' presents until – I had to go out and attend to my pony, who was there, really and truly there, the promise, the beginning of a happy double life. And – I went and looked to make sure – there was the saddle, too, and the bridle.

But that Christmas, which my father had planned so carefully, was it the best or the worst I ever knew? He often asked me that; I never could answer as a boy. I think now that it was both. It covered the whole distance from broken-hearted misery to bursting happiness – too fast. A grown-up could hardly have stood it.

CHUT THE KANGAROO

Dorothy Cottrell

*When the three men had finished skinning their game – two kangaroos –
they took a last look around. Suddenly one of them saw the infant "joey"
whose mother had been killed the night before.*

"Jove!" said the man. "There's a little fellow!"

He pounced upon Chut, who simply shrank into himself
and waited for the last spasm of the terror which was death.

"He's a little beauty," said the man. "I'm going to take him
home to my wife." He held Chut up ridiculously by the scruff
of the neck and poked him with his finger. Then the man
looked puzzled. "He's all scratched and he's been cut across
the back – looks like an eagle's had him . . . Say, I guess he
must have belonged to the doe that got away last night! Poor
little nipper!"

"Let's take him and give him a drink!" the other men
suggested. Gathering up the skins, they moved off round the
head of the dam, Chut hanging limp and hopeless under the
big man's arm.

At the camp, back over the ridge, there was discussion as to
how the baby should be fed and some facetious suggestions of
sending for Dr. Holt's Book on Infant Feeding. Then the first
man said: "He won't drink unless he's upside down . . ." So
they got an old pair of trousers and tied a knot in one leg at
the knee, and hung the trousers to a tree limb by the back

strap. Then they held Chut up before it. He looked at it in confusion.

"Better let him get in himself," said the big man. He gave Chut a friendly pinch. It worked. Instinctively Chut grasped the edge of the trousers, lowered his head, and bracing his hoppers against the big man's stomach, turned his dexterous somersault into the warm depths of the leg! Once again he was swinging as a kangaroo should swing. He was enclosed; safe. He gave a feeble, twittering chitter.

One of the other men stepped forward and presented him with the end of a bit of insulating rubber, from which the wire had been withdrawn, and whose other end was in a tin of milk.

Chut sucked, sucked again. Milk was in his mouth. He gave little ticking sounds of bliss, and, still drinking, he fell asleep in the maternal embrace of the trouser leg.

Chut's wound healed. The men were good to him. He learned the new smells of fire-smoke, and potatoes roasting in ashes; the mellow smell of coffee and the sharp tang of tea, the odours of frizzling bacon and grilling chops; of tobacco smoke by a camp fire under stars; and the sneeziness of raw flour, and the smell of men. He learned that fire was hot and kerosene nasty. His ears attuned themselves to new sounds, for the men were as noisy as the wilderness was silent. Clatter of plates, loud jests and louder laughter, galloping of horses and clanging music of horse-bells, ceased to appal him.

When, after a month's work on the lower run, the big man returned home, Chut went with him, swinging securely in one leg of a pair of old trousers attached to the man's saddle. Arrived at the small, tree-set homestead, the man was met by his young wife; and Chut, observing the meeting through a cigarette hole in the trouser leg, sensed that it was affectionate.

"I've brought you home a baby!" the big man said, untying the old trousers from the pommel of the saddle, and handing them to her – one of the legs showing plumply bulged. She took the garment hesitatingly, peering into the top, perceived Chut where he waited in bright-eyed, velvet-furred minuteness, and exclaimed: "Oh, the darling, sweet, tiny thing!"

The man dismounted, and stepped up to her.

"He is so little!" she said. "And so soft and fat."

At that the man took her in his arms.

"What," she said, "will we call him?"

But, squeezed between the big man and his wife, Chut was very uncomfortable. He gave a surprisingly loud and indignant cry of protest. "Chut! Chut! Chut-ch-ch-ch-ch!"

So he was called "Chut", which prior to this time had simply been his staple of conversation and announcement of his presence.

During the day he followed the girl about like a little dog. At night he slept in the trousers which swung by the big outside fireplace – these habiliments coming to be known as "Chut's pants".

He would come when the woman called him, and somersault neatly into her lap as she sat on the steps. There, lying on his back, he took his supper to the accompaniment of small kicks of pleasure.

He was also promoted to all the dignity of a real baby's bottle instead of the bit of insulating tube fastened to a condensed milk tin with which the men had nourished him in camp. The dogs were introduced to him one by one, it being forcefully explained to them that he was taboo.

There was soft green grass in which he might roll, and many trailing pepper trees beneath which to play small solitary games. In short, his world was eminently satisfactory – save for one thing.

There was at the homestead a ridiculously fat, excessively bumptious lamb, by name William Mutton. To William had belonged the baby's bottle before Chut took it over, and William harboured a dark and bitter resentment at the loss of his bottle. He was an incredibly greedy lamb. And, although fed to repletion, he was forever sucking at the woman's fingers, at her apron strings, at the tassels of blinds – anything. A moment after having eaten until he could eat no more, he called pitifully of his semi-starvation. To see anyone else eat appeared to cause him pain.

"That lamb," said the big man, "is not, I fear, of a generous turn of mind. He might even be described as a little grasping."

At least, to see Chut being nourished appeared to sear the very soul of William Mutton. Chut had been eager to be friendly. Upon one of the first occasions when he had ventured on a little walk by himself, he had come upon the lamb around a trailing pepper branch. The baleful gleam in William Mutton's eye meant nothing to him. All he saw was a creature of approximately his own size who might possibly want to sport a little.

Chut drew himself up to his now twenty-five-inch height, and standing poised upon the arch of his lower tail and the tips of his toes he gave a few stiff, bouncing little sidehops – the kangaroo's invitation to play.

"Chut!" he remarked affably. "Chut! Ch-ch!"

William's head dropped lower. He focused evilly upon the cream-velvet rotundity of Chut's stomach. Then, with a malevolent "Baa", he charged upon the little kangaroo.

His round woolly head met Chut's silk-furred stomach with a resonant plop. Chut grunted and fell, kicking, while William strolled triumphantly about his business without even deigning to look back.

After that he took especial pains to make the little kangaroo's life wretched. He specialized in knocking Chut down from different directions and in varying localities. He learned his victim's weaknesses and played upon them . . .

Persistent persecution will, of course, develop wariness in the most confiding creature, and as Chut grew older he became harder to catch. On the other hand, if William's butts became less frequent, they became harder: for William was a particularly hefty young sheep and in addition he was growing horns – only nubby buds as yet, but distinctly uncomfortable when applied to Chut's person.

Then, about the time that, greatly to his own surprise, Chut outgrew his trouser leg, the big man, whose name Chut now knew was Tom Henton, brought in two little does who were just a shade smaller than Chut had been at the time of his capture.

And the woman whom everyone but Tom Henton called Mrs. Henton christened them Zodie and Blue Baby, and Chut promptly adopted them both. He would sit for twenty minutes at a time chitting and whispering into the mouths of their sleeping bags. He nosed them, and pulled in a manly, masterful way at their ears.

When they were old enough to come out to play, he romped with them, and at times put his little arms round both their necks so that the three small heads were drawn close together. Then he led them upon little gallops beneath the trees.

Of the two little does, Blue Baby was his darling. For as gentlemen allegedly prefer blondes, so male kangaroos seem melted by a blue tone in a lady's fur: experienced old kangaroo

hunters having often noticed that amongst all the mouse-hued harem an "old man" will make a pet of a blue doe.

And Blue Baby was furred in an exquisite shade of smoke blue, brighter than the bluest of squirrel fur, and her stomach and chest were clear, cream-velvet. Her slender little tail, hoppers and hands, were dark, her eyes dark and dewy-soft. But for some reason she was slightly lame.

She could travel all right on her hoppers and hands, but when she attempted to hop in an upright position she stumbled and fell. Hence she was always left behind in the races. And Chut would always circle back for her, and pass and repass her – as though he did not want her to be left out.

When she too outgrew the trousers, he slept with one little arm about her neck, their attitudes touchingly like those of sleeping children.

71

As an evil shadow on the sunshine of young romance hovered the malevolent-eyed Mutton, always ready to charge upon the unguarded Chut and knock the wind out of him.

But Chut was growing miraculously fast now. His chubbiness had gone from him, likewise the legginess of youth that followed it. He was nowhere near his full growth – would not reach it for a long time yet – but he was strong-boned, erect, with the muscles swelling deeply beneath the skin of his forearms and back. When he drew himself up, he was almost as tall as Mrs. Henton. But at her call his great body still somersaulted innocently into her lap, and, when he could inveigle her into giving it to him, he still adored his bottle. He still lay on his back in the sun and played with his toes, and he still had an infantile attachment for the pair of trousers which had been his foster-mother.

After the manner of kangaroos he was consumingly curious. He wanted to see everything. He tasted everything, and loved bread and sugar.

Gentle and awkward on the slippery oilcloth, the three kangaroos would come begging about the dinner table for pieces of sugared bread, which they had been taught to carry outside before eating – although they often fell to temptation and snatched little bites as they went.

One day they had just got their precious sweetened bread, and carried it out beneath the big pepper tree, when the marauding Mutton bore down upon them.

Chut and Zodie hopped out of the way, still holding their crusts, but Blue Baby was clumsy and in her agitation she dropped her bread.

Had William Mutton contented himself with merely taking the bread, it is doubtful if Chut would have noticed, but William, who in the past had always confined his attacks to Chut, suddenly decided that Blue Baby would do as well. And, with an evil "Baa", he charged her – sending her sprawling to the grass, chittering little exclamations of fright!

Chut looked up. Blue Baby chittered more alarmedly.

Chut dropped his bread and drew himself up on to toes and

lower tail-arch, and made a few little bouncing dancing steps: a kangaroo's invitation to play or fight.

William Mutton had seized Blue Baby's bit of bread. Blue Baby still lay on her back in the grass, too astonished and frightened to rise.

Chut danced up to the sheep, his arms hanging out from his sides like a belligerent man's, his ribs expanded.

"Chut!" he cried harshly. "Chut! Chut! Chut!"

"Baa!" said William Mutton, contemptuously masticating. Next moment he was grabbed by the backwool, and one of Chut's long hind toes kicked him dexterously in the side, tearing out a hunk of wool as it ripped downward.

Like most bullies, William was an arrant coward. He bleated and leapt for safety. Chut clawed for his fat rump as he went, and pulled out more wool. William gathered pulsing momentum of baa-punctuated bounds. And Chut followed him, trying vainly for another kick — for anything as low as a sheep is a most awkward thing for a kangaroo to fight.

William fled wildly, crying for undeserved help. The swimming pool lay before them. At its edge William, who dreaded water, tried to wheel, and at the same moment gave a foolish, prancing rear-up!

This was fatal. A kangaroo cannot kick well unless it can embrace the thing it is kicking. William's semi-leap brought

73

him to the perfect height for Chut's best attentions. Chut's hands clutched the miserable sheep's neck, his strong-muscled arms tightened like virgin rubber as he clasped the writhing form of Mutton to his chest. With "chuts" and nickers of rage he delivered a whirlwind of kicks to his victim's stomach.

They were his first fighting kicks, and poorly directed – which was as well for William – but they drew bleats and wool at each application.

Then Chut lost his balance, released his hold for a moment, and William Mutton made a frantic leap for safety – into the pool!

Tom Henton, who had been an amused and astonished spectator of the fight, fished him out again. He emerged a sadder and wiser sheep, to whom a kangaroo's stomach was forever after invisible.

But Chut had tasted the hot wine of his own strength. He wanted someone to wrestle with! During the next days he hopped pompously about the garden enclosure, with his arms swinging a little out from his sides, his chest expanded and his spine curving backward with his erectness. He stood in front of Tom Henton as he came in of an evening, and made little sparring, sideward hops on the extreme tips of his toes and ridged arch of his lower-tail.

One night the man laughed, saying: "All right then!" and put on boxing gloves to spar with the great young kangaroo. Mrs. Henton had viewed the proceeding with alarm, for a kangaroo can disembowel a man or dog with a single scythe-rip of his hooked foot. But it was soon obvious that Chut fully understood the playful nature of the battle. He would no more have thought of letting his strength go than the man would have dreamed of putting his full weight behind a blow to Chut's jaw.

They clinched and swayed, they sparred and side-stepped, until Tom leapt back to wipe the sweat from his streaming face, and Chut panted, and cooled his arms by licking them to the semblance of dark rubber.

After this they wrestled almost every evening, and so

"boxing" was added to Chut's tricks. At the end of a match, if he had "played" well, he got his little bit of bread and sugar – which he held in both hands and smeared disgustingly about his face.

It happened that the summer had been a very busy one for Tom Henton, and so he had engaged a "yardman" to look after the cows, and the wood-chopping, and the home vegetable garden. The youth who performed these duties was not prepossessing, his manner alternating between over-familiarity and sullenness, while his progress was exasperatingly deliberate. A seemingly permanent cigarette drooped from his lower lip, and he did not remove it as he spoke.

Still, labour was hard to get, and Tom Henton decided to keep the man until after the shearing.

William Mutton, who had no decent pride, would follow the yardman about in the hope of sneaking something from the fowls' bucket, but Chut ignored the youth's existence.

At least he ignored it until the shearing-time came.

The shearing shed and the sheep yards were some half-mile from the house, but dust clouds stirred up from the drafting pens had come to Chut's nostrils with exciting scents of heat and sheep trailing from them. He caught far, murmurous bleatings, stockwhip cracks, distant shoutings . . .

And Chut wanted to go and see the shearing! He plainly indicated as much as Tom Henton was riding out of a morning: placing one horny, confiding hand upon the man's stirrup in hint that he was coming too. When, in spite of this, he was left behind, he hopped up and down inside the enclosure fence, thumping his twenty-pound tail deliberately and loudly upon the ground as an intimation of his extreme displeasure and agitation.

Tom Henton had given very definite instructions that the big kangaroo was not to be let out during shearing. He didn't want any tricks played upon Chut, and shearer-men have an odd sense of humour. Also there was always the chance of a sudden fright temporarily stampeding the kangaroo into the bush, and there he might be shot in mistake for a wild 'roo.

"Keep the gates shut," said Tom to the yardman. "And be dead sure they're fastened!" The youth spat and said "O.K.," but he had already resolved to take Chut down to the shed and stage a demonstration fight for a shilling-a-man admission.

To do this he waited until a Sunday afternoon, when Tom Henton was away bringing in sheep for Monday's "run", and Mrs. Henton was lying down asleep.

Chut was also dozing under a pepper tree, with his legs sticking absurdly skyward, when the yardman whispered his name and enticed him with bread. But he took no notice until he saw the man open the gate. Then he followed, and continued following all the way to the shed: hopping behind the yardman's pony. At the shed he was embarrassed by the number of people and by the great wool-smelling iron rooms.

And, because the yardman was at least familiar, Chut followed him more closely still.

The yardman collected his shillings, and then led the big, puzzled kangaroo into the wool room, while the audience seated itself upon the stacked bales of wool.

The yardman fastened on Chut's gloves and put on gloves himself: then he stepped out in a fighting attitude, saying: "Come on, Boy!"

Chut didn't want to come on, however. He was rather frightened by the laughter, the voices, and the smoke haze. Also he was particular about the people with whom he fought. His boxing was a love-game he played with Tom Henton.

"Put 'em up!" said the yardman, tapping Chut lightly upon the cheek. Chut sat far back on his haunches and chutted offendedly: a small sound in appealing contrast to his size. The man danced up and down before him and poked him in the ribs. Chut protested with dignity, but made no attempt to fight.

Grumbling began amongst the members of the audience.

"Hey, where's my shilling?" "Aw, I'm going home." "This is a dead show!" "*That* the best he can do?"

The yardman began to lose his temper. The fool beast

fought quick enough when he wanted to! He was going to fight now! He hit Chut rather ungently in the lower ribs. Chut grunted and looked about with great soft eyes – appealing for fair play! He was not hurting this man, and the man was getting rough with him!

Still he obviously had no intention of sparring. He was a picture of gentle, slightly pompous, and much-offended courtesy. He looked about for Tom or Mrs. Henton . . .

"Garn! He's no fighter!" yelled the men. "Where's them shillin's?"

The yardman was hot, nervous and exasperated. His audience was threatening to walk out on him. Unnoticed by any of the spectators, he snatched the live cigarette from his lips, and holding it hidden in his glove he pressed the glowing tip upon Chut's sensitive nose. Pressed it hard, twisted it.

The sequel happened so quickly that no one was sure of just how Chut got the silly gloves off. But the next second he was holding the screaming yardman in his powerful hug, and, having torn the youth's trousers off, was operating on his shirt-tail to the accompaniment of a ripping, rag-bag sort of sound!

As the shirt vanished, Chut's great-toe plied artistically for a hold upon the yardman's abdomen. With his forehand he clawed the yardman's hair. His eyes had a new, murderous light. He shook and bent the man in his embrace! . . .

Then half the men in the shed were on him. Beating at him with rails, prodding him with wool-hooks.

He dropped the frantic and badly clawed yardman, and wheeled – to receive a bewildering rain of blows!

His swift anger was already over. All he wanted was to go home. He burst through the threatening circle and hopped majestically out of the wool-room door, gathering momentum as he went, and moving homeward, not with the frantic thirty-feet-at-a-bound of a frightened doe, but rhythmically covering a steady fifteen feet at a hop. One man fired after him, but the shots went wide.

It was at this stage that Tom Henton rode up to the shed, to

be horrified at the tale of Chut's ferocity and the spectacle of the bleeding man. With relief he found that no vital injury had been done, but it was with a heavy heart that he at last rode home. The shearers, none of whom had observed the cigarette outrage, had assured him that the yardman had simply been inviting Chut to a friendly sparring bout!

If Chut was going to make unprovoked attacks like that, he was not safe . . .

Mrs. Henton was likewise shocked at the account of the yardman's injuries. But she refused to believe that Chut's anger had been unprovoked.

"We simply couldn't shoot him!" she cried. "Why, if he could tell us what happened, he could very likely explain everything! Oh Tom, he is so dear and funny!"

"We can't get his side of it," said the man. "And the fact remains that if he hadn't been beaten off he might have killed someone."

"You *can't* shoot him!"

"I can't see how we can keep him. I'd be afraid for you, honey. Afraid to have him loose around – and I'd sooner shoot him than cage him."

"I know he wouldn't hurt anyone unless they hurt him!" she cried. But Tom looked away with troubled face.

"You know how we would feel if there was an accident," he said.

"Well, don't do it yet – after dinner – not yet."

The evening meal passed in heavy silence. They were both thinking about what would have to be done. As they rose from the table the woman began to cry. She said: "Oh Tom, you can't!"

"I'll have to," said the man, still looking away from her. Suddenly she took his arm.

"Come and see him, before we make up our minds!"

They passed along the veranda to the old outside fireplace. Chut was lying on his back beside the faded and shredded remains of the trousers that had mothered him. His eyes were soft and sad with dreams.

As the man and woman looked down at him, he reached up great arms to catch his great toe.

With tears and laughter mingling in her voice, the woman said: "Oh, Tom, he can't be dangerous! Look at him!"

"He doesn't look it," said the man, tears gleaming in his eyes.

Just then the girl fell swiftly to her knees, her fingers searching the velvet fur just above the kangaroo's quivering nose. "Look!" she cried. "Look!"

The man held the lamp down. On Chut's nose there was a small, deep, raw pit, eaten into the flesh. About the edges of the rawness the hair was singed and burnt.

"Couldn't that have been done by a cigarette?" she questioned.

"You bet it was!" he replied.

"Well," she said, "that's *his* side of the story for you, Tom!" Then she reached down and clasped her arms about Chut's neck. "Oh, I am so glad! So glad!"

They stood up.

"I," said the man, "am sorry . . ."

"What do you *mean*?" questioned the girl.

"I'm sorry Chut's done such a good job with the yardman that he hasn't left me a chance!" said Tom Henton, his fingers lingering about the swell of his bicep.

Later the girl slipped back and gave Chut a whole half-loaf of bread with melted sugar. He ate it placidly and blissfully, with small tickings of pleasure. Sugar ran down his chin and got into his fur. He was soon perfectly horrible with sugar and covered with crumbs. Nevertheless, his mistress stooped and kissed him.

JUJU THE JACKDAW
A true story

Hazel Wilkinson

Every spring the baby birds, jackdaws and pigeons fell down the chimneys of the town hall where my father worked, and every spring he brought them home to be raised until they could fly away. When he arrived with the small cardboard boxes, we would lift the lids and look inside to see the large beaks open as the baby birds strained upwards, hoping for food. Each bird in its cardboard box would stay on the draining board while my mother and father behaved like the parent birds and kept up a constant supply of food. They would put a little blob of brown bread and milk, or chopped hard-boiled egg, or little grubs from the garden on a spoon handle, and use the handle, as the parent birds used their beaks, to push the food into the gaping beak. After a week or so the little bird would be able to feed itself and would have grown a few proper feathers to replace the scruffy grey down that had earlier covered much of the pinkish-grey skin. Soon it would go to live in a larger wooden box with a wire-netting front that was placed in the back yard. This was the time for fast growth and in no time at all the bird would begin to hop about. It was funny to see them try to fly; often they needed lessons, so we would put them on a high fence and encourage them to fly towards a dish of food. They never seemed to be able to take off from the ground but, with help, each tentative flutter got longer and the awkward flapping changed to a confident flight.

When they seemed to be independent, we left the cage door open permanently and they were free to go. They came back for an occasional meal of bread and milk, but left us when they were about six weeks old to lead their own bird life; they needed no further attentions from human beings.

Juju was different. At first he seemed just like the other little birds. He was scrawny and scraggy and he squawked loudly, he ate ravenously and flapped his stumpy wings awkwardly; however, he did learn to feed himself and to fly, and then his cage door was left open, and this is where he was different. He didn't want to fly away!

His name came from the year in which he was born, 1935, the Silver Jubilee Year, and also from the fact that it was easy to believe that he was involved in black magic. He showed no signs of leaving and had obviously decided that he was one of the family. My mother found him useful, since he warned her when my father was coming home from work. At the appropriate time Juju would begin to fly higher and higher above the house, and as soon as he spotted my father coming home across the field, he flew off, met him with joyful squawks, nibbled my father's ear in a gentle manner and rode home on his shoulder. With such accurate warning, my mother could serve supper at exactly the right moment.

My sisters and I enjoyed our unique pet, but didn't enjoy all of his attentions. When we went into the garden in the summer, Juju would follow us and peck at the little fair hairs on our legs. He had the typical jackdaw delight in shining objects and would take away anything small and glittery that he could carry. He would fly in at the windows, and on one occasion was suspected of removing a silver christening spoon. He was proved to be the thief when he was seen to fly away with my sister Janet's tiny silver spectacles. My father tracked down his untidy nest in the top of a drainpipe, and there were the spectacles and the spoon, *and* the silver top of a scent bottle, all resting in a litter of silver foil and bits of tin and glass.

Although Juju was quite capable of finding his own food, he always came home for his supper when he heard a tin mug rattle on the concrete yard. His usual snack was brown bread and milk with crumbs of cheese, so it was quite a problem when we were all going away on a summer holiday. The dilemma was solved when my father made Juju a small travelling box which hung from one of the struts holding up the roof canvas of our old Humber touring car. Juju sat there swaying calmly and surveying the world with his bright, black eyes; he didn't seem at all perturbed by his strange surroundings. As soon as we got to our holiday chalet and had unloaded the car, Juju was allowed out to stretch his wings; we all held our breath while he took off and flew out of sight, but he soon returned to his temporary home. Just as we spent our time exploring our new surroundings, so Juju flew off on regular exploring trips. One morning when we were all sitting outside in the sunshine eating our breakfast we heard our neighbours on the other side of a tall hedge say, "Oh look, here's that bird again! Have we got some food for him?" And then we found out what a very clever bird Juju was! He went to most of the families round about and was fed and petted by them all. When that holiday ended, Juju rode happily home again in his special box, and whenever we went away we took him with us, so he became a much-travelled bird.

Juju lived with us until 1941. That was when we children were evacuated to a family in Wales. My father had been in the army for some time and my mother went to join him. Juju went to Wiltshire with my mother and father, and it was when my father had to live in a huge army camp that Juju must have become confused. Although he was a very clever bird, it must have been extremely difficult to pick out one man in khaki amongst thousands of other khaki-clad men. Juju obviously decided to look for his family back at his old home in Hertfordshire. He disappeared from the camp in

Wiltshire and after several months one of our neighbours was surprised to find him sitting on her washing line. He surprised her even more when he said "Hello!" The poor lady dropped her washing and dashed indoors to recover. Other neighbours saw Juju flying about our house until he must have realized that we were away. We are sure that then he went to spend the rest of his life with other jackdaws. There is always a large colony of them in some tall trees at the bottom of the field that my father used to cross, so we think that the ones we see nowadays are Juju's relatives and descendants, but none of them ever says "Hello" to us!

THE CHRISTMAS CAT

Adèle Geras

The children in Miss Hunt's class were making a Christmas picture big enough to cover the whole of one wall. Some things had already been pasted on to a background of thick, blue paper: a fireplace cut out of wallpaper with red and orange painted flames licking up towards the mantelpiece, a Christmas tree with milk-bottle tops and tinsel for decoration, drawings of presents under the tree, presents with real ribbon bows stuck on them. The picture was almost ready. Outlines of armchairs were going up today, and pink curtains and balls of cotton wool to be snow on the painted windows. Miss Hunt was sitting at Joanna's table, showing her and Eddie how to make the cat that was going to lie curled up beside the fire.

"Here you are, then, Joanna dear. Cut very carefully around the shape I've drawn. The head first, then the body. Be careful with the scissors, now. Then, Eddie, you can put the glue on to the cardboard shapes and you can both stick it down. Right?"

"Yes, Miss Hunt," Eddie said, and "Yes," Joanna added absent-mindedly.

She was too busy looking at the furry material on the table to pay proper attention. She stroked it one way, then another, seeing how the light lay on it in lines and ridges, counting the different shades of brown that flowed through it like waves. It made her think of Pobble, who used to be her cat, but who

was dead now and buried under a rose bush in the garden. A car had hit him and he had died, and although Maggie, her sister, and her father and mother had said she could have another cat, Joanna didn't want one. When they asked her why she didn't, she wouldn't tell them, but it was because she was frightened of the new cat being knocked over by a car. If it happened once, she thought, it could happen again.

This cat, now, this cloth cat that she was cutting out, could live on the wall of her room and be safe.

"I'm going to ask Miss Hunt if I can have this cat," she said. "When it's the holidays and we take this picture down."

"So am I," said Eddie. "I'm making it with you. It's my cat, just as much as yours."

"But I'm cutting the cat. You're only glueing and sticking."

"Doesn't matter. I still want it."

"Well, you won't have it."

"Will."

"Won't."

Their voices rose above the murmur in the classroom. Tears gathered in Joanna's eyes.

"Now, now, children," Miss Hunt said. "What's this noise

then? Oh, that's lovely, Joanna and Eddie. It's going to look really splendid!"

"Please, Miss," Joanna said, "Eddie says he wants to take the cat home in the holidays and I do as well. Please may I take it? Oh, please."

"We'll see, Joanna, we'll see. Don't worry about it now. There's two weeks still this term, and it's staying up till the very last day. Then I'll see who's taking it home."

"I hope I get it," Eddie said, as they stuck the cat shape down. "It'll be a pet. We're not allowed real pets in our flats."

"I don't like real cats," said Joanna. "I cut this one out, so it's mine. Miss Hunt will give it to me. I bet you anything she will."

Eddie said nothing. He scowled at Joanna for the rest of the morning whenever he caught her looking at him.

After dinner, the cat was stuck up on the wall and everyone clapped and said "ooh" and "aah" and agreed that it was the best bit of the whole picture. Joanna didn't know what to think. Eddie was her friend and she didn't like him scowling

at her, but she knew that she wanted the cat more than she
had ever wanted anything.

"So it's not fair," Joanna told her sister. "Is it, Maggie?"

"He helped to make it," Maggie said.

"But only the cardboard and the sticking. I did the fur. It was
hard too. The ears and everything. And I stuck on the pipe-
cleaners for whiskers. And one of the eyes. And anyways . . ."

"Yes?"

"It'll cheer me up."

"I didn't know you needed cheering up. Aren't you excited
about moving to another house?"

"Not really."

"Why not? Don't you like the new house?"

"It's very nice. It's bigger than this one, isn't it?"

"Yes, it is. You'll have a proper room, not a little box. I can't
wait."

"But won't you miss all the things you leave behind here?"

"I'm not leaving anything behind here, though, am I?" said
Maggie. "A big truck is going to come and take every single
thing in this house – all the toys and books and furniture and
even the carpets and curtains, and take them to the new
house."

"Really?" Joanna couldn't believe it. For nights and nights
she hadn't slept properly, worrying about never seeing her
toys again, or her bed, wondering whether she would like
sleeping in the bed she had seen in the new house, and would
those toys be as dear to her as her own which she would be
leaving behind. She understood now. Why had no one told
her before? Why had no one explained that they were going
to take all their things with them? Why had she never asked?
Because it had never occurred to her. For weeks she had
carried what felt like a hard lump of pain somewhere inside
her and now it had disappeared, just like magic, when Maggie
said those words.

"But," Joanna asked, "how will our things fit into the new
house, if they leave their things behind?"

"They don't leave their things," Maggie said impatiently. "They'll take them to the house they're moving into. Everyone takes their own stuff when they change houses. Don't you see?"

"Yes, I do now," Joanna giggled. "Before, I thought it was like musical chairs. You know, everybody changing places. Oh, I hope I get the cat. There'll be lots of room to stick it up in the new house. You should see it, Maggie. It's just like a real cat. The fur is lovely. It feels real. And it's lots of different colours of brown."

"Not as good as a real cat, though," Maggie said. "Why don't you ask for a kitten for Christmas? A real one? You can't play with a cat that's stuck up on a wall."

"Yes, you can." Joanna stuck her bottom lip out. "You can."

"How? What can you do with it? You can't feed it, or watch it run about or anything. It's stupid."

"You can. It's not stupid." Joanna looked at the floor. She thought: you can talk to it, and stroke it, and watch it sleeping, up there on the wall, and it'll never get lost or hurt itself and nothing bad will ever happen to it. She glanced across at her sister, about to explain, but Maggie had picked up her book and was reading it and chewing her bookmark, which meant that she was concentrating and didn't want to be disturbed.

Three days before the end of term, the frost came. Dead leaves in the playground looked as though they had been dipped in icing sugar, the green railings were edged with white powder, dancing pinpricks of glitter in the thin sunlight. A huge puddle had frozen over, and all the big children were skating on it, making patterns on the ice with the heels of their shoes, pushing the smaller children to the edges where the ice was cloudy and cracked.

"It's our playground," Eddie shouted. "Our playground and our puddle and our ice. Why don't you play in your own playground?"

"Because there's no ice in ours, stupid," said one big boy.

"Well, we're allowed to skate, too," Eddie muttered and began to slip gingerly about on the edge of the ice.

"Come on, Eddie," Tim and Pralad shouted.

"Come on!" Joanna yelled and Julie jumped up and down beside her.

Kathy and Salima followed Eddie on to the ice. Soon, half a dozen of Miss Hunt's children were sliding about. Joanna tried to, but her shoes had thick, rubber soles and she couldn't move at all, so she hopped about to keep warm and watched the others. Kathy kept falling over. Her skirt would be wet. So would her gloves. The bigger children had gone. Eddie was twirling in a circle, pushing himself round on one foot, both his hands held high above his head, like a dancer. Breath curled out of his mouth in thick, misty loops and spirals and hung in the blue-white air. Then he gave a big push with his leg and lost his balance. He wobbled and teetered like a giraffe about to do the splits and then came crashing down on to the icy concrete. Everyone rushed to see what had happened, crowding around him.

Eddie was crying and groaning.

"Get somebody!" Pralad yelled.

"Can you walk?"

"Are you all right?"

"Does it hurt?"

Joanna ran to where Mrs Johnston was standing, right on the other side of the playground.

"Please, Miss, Eddie's fallen over. Please come and see. He can't get up at all," Joanna gasped.

Mrs Johnston ran to the ice-puddle.

"Can you move your leg at all, Eddie?" she said.

"No," wailed Eddie. "No . . . o."

Mrs Johnston turned to Joanna. "Please go in and ask Mrs Evans to telephone for an ambulance. Tell her I think Eddie may have hurt his leg quite badly."

Joanna ran. Glancing towards the playground as she went into school, she saw that Mrs Johnston had taken off her sheepskin coat and covered Eddie with it.

Miss Hunt came out to wait for the ambulance. The bell had gone, but the children were allowed to wait and see the ambulance arrive. They stood at the railings, craning their necks.

"It'll come from over there," said Kathy.

"No it won't. The hospital's that way."

"We'll hear it first, anyway," said Tim. "It'll have its siren going. I bet it will."

"There it is," Joanna shouted. "It hasn't got its siren on. It's got a blue light flashing on top."

The ambulance drove quickly up to the gates. Two men carrying a stretcher ran across the playground to where Eddie was lying. Joanna and the other children watched as they lifted Eddie carefully on to the stretcher and covered him with a red blanket. Miss Hunt held his hand. She was going to the hospital with him, to look after him.

"Don't worry, kids," said one of the men. "They'll patch him up, good as new."

Mrs Johnston put her coat back on. The children stared at the tail lights of the ambulance as it disappeared round the corner.

"Go to your classroom now, children," said Mrs Johnston. "Mrs Evans will come and sit with you till dinner time."

The day went very slowly. Dinner time came and there was no sign of Eddie, nor of Miss Hunt. Mrs Evans told them stories and they drew pictures on rough paper and stared at the apricot sun through the frost-forests on the window panes. Just before home time, Miss Hunt came in.

"Children, I'm afraid poor Eddie has broken his leg. Not a very bad break, but still, he'll be in plaster all over the holidays and for a week or two after that. I know how sorry you all are, and tomorrow we'll make him a lovely card and send it to him. Now go and get your coats on and remember, no more skating on that puddle, please."

"Yes, Miss," whispered the children and went to fetch their coats more quietly than usual.

Next morning, Joanna said to Miss Hunt: "Will you be able to send the cat home to Eddie? I think he should have it now. It'll cheer him up."

"That's a kind thought, Joanna. Will you write a little note to go with it?"

Joanna wrote: "Dear Eddie. Here is the cat. His name is Brownie. I hope you are better soon. Love from Joanna."

Part of her felt happy because she knew how pleased Eddie would be and because she understood how awful it was to be stuck at home for weeks and weeks. And she felt sad, too. She had lost another pet. Grown attached to it and then lost it. I

93

hate cats, Joanna thought. I never, ever want to see another cat, not ever.

The day they moved house, it was snowing. Joanna opened the back door to see how deep it was. If it went on snowing all night, tomorrow there might be enough for a snowman. The garage roof was polka-dotted with white, and flakes were sticking to the fans of brown twigs on every tree. It was nearly dark, but the snow had its own brightness and its own silence. Suddenly the silence was broken. Joanna heard, from somewhere, the thin miaowing of a cat. She closed the door quickly.

Joanna's mother said, "Can you hear a cat miaowing?"

"Yes, Mum. I expect it's a cat from one of the other houses."

"Sounds desperate to me. Did you see anything, when you looked out just now?"

"No, nothing."

"Well, have another look, please. It's too cold out there for a cat to be wandering about."

Joanna opened the door and a little brown kitten streaked past her legs and hid itself behind the boiler.

"Oh, Mum, look it's gone behind the boiler now. We'll never get it out."

Joanna's mother smiled, and took a bottle of milk out of the fridge.

Joanna was beginning to like the new house. At first, it had been empty and echoing and all their things were piled into boxes in the hall. The chairs had looked strange in a different place, and Joanna's little bed seemed lost in her new, bigger room. But now all the pictures were up, all her toys had been unpacked, and everything had begun to look as though it had always been there.

Especially Cat. It was the morning of Christmas Eve. He lay next to the Christmas tree, on top of a heap of presents. Pink light fell on him, filtering through the red and yellow glass flowers of the hall window. Joanna and Maggie had gone

round all the houses in the street to see if he had a home, but no one had claimed him.

"He's claimed us," Maggie said. "We'll have to keep him."

"But what if he gets knocked over by a car?" said Joanna.

"We don't live on the main road any more," Maggie said. "He'll be much safer here. There's hardly any traffic at all. He'll be fine, don't worry."

Joanna was beginning to think that perhaps he would be. When he lay curled up, he looked just like Brownie. When Eddie was better, he could come and visit and play with Cat. Joanna ran her hands along Cat's back, rubbing his fur the wrong way. He opened a green eye, yawned a wide pink yawn and rippled himself into a different position.

"You'll be all right, Cat," Joanna said. "I'll look after you."

A PET FOR MRS ARBUCKLE

Gwenda Smyth

Mrs Emmeline Arbuckle needed a pet.

She needed a pet to look after and talk to.

She had Mr A. but he didn't need much looking after and he watched the football on TV instead of listening.

Mrs Arbuckle told the gingernut cat from down the street that she needed a pet.

"Well, of course," said the gingernut cat. "You must advertise."

So Mrs Arbuckle put an advertisement in the newspaper: WANTED – A PET FOR A SWEET OLD LADY. VERY GOOD HOME.

She received eleven letters from animals all over the world.

"Wow!" said Mrs Arbuckle. "Eleven applications! What happens now?"

"Now you must interview them," said the gingernut cat from down the street.

"I'll come too, in case you need a second opinion."

Mrs Arbuckle packed her overnight bag and put on her boots and her shawl.

"We're off," she said – and they went to Mexico to interview an armadillo. He had scaly skin and a very nice nature.

"I'd make a lovely pet," said the armadillo. "I could curl myself into a ball and roll along beside you when you go cycling. The neighbours would be amazed."

"There's a lot to be said for amazing the neighbours," agreed Mrs Arbuckle.

But the gingernut cat said, "Do you want a ball or a pet? Because, if you want a ball, let's go to a toyshop."

"I see what you mean," said Mrs Arbuckle.

So they said goodbye to the armadillo – and went to the centre of Africa to interview a giraffe.

"I'll be with you in a minute," said the giraffe, and he went on nibbling the leaves at the top of a thorn-tree.

Mrs Arbuckle and the gingernut cat climbed up the thorn-tree to talk to the giraffe.

"I'd be a stimulating pet," said the giraffe. "I could see over the fence and tell you what was happening next door."

"I'd like that," said Mrs Arbuckle.

"But look at it this way," argued the gingernut cat. "Do you want all the tops of your trees eaten off?"

"No, I suppose not," said Mrs Arbuckle.

So they said goodbye to the giraffe – and went to Patagonia to interview a llama. The llama was nowhere to be seen, but they saw two eyes peeping through the bushes.

"Won't you come out?" invited Mrs Arbuckle.

"I'm shy," said the llama, but he shyly came out from the bushes, and so did his father and mother and sisters and brothers and aunts and uncles and cousins.

"We're very loving creatures," said the llama, "and we need a change of scene. Australia would suit us fine."

"All of you?" asked Mrs Arbuckle.

"Oh, I couldn't come without the family," explained the llama.

"What fun to have a garden full of llamas!" cried Mrs Arbuckle.

"A joke is a joke," said the gingernut cat, "and a pet is a pet, and a herd is a herd."

"You're right, of course," agreed Mrs Arbuckle.

So they said goodbye to the llamas – and went to California to see a whale. Mrs Arbuckle put on her swimming costume and her bathing cap, her flippers and her snorkel, and went out on a raft to meet the whale.

"If you took me home," said the whale, "you'd be famous overnight. I'd probably be the only pet whale in the street."

"I like your type," said Mrs Arbuckle, looking him up and down. "There'd be something very comforting about having a whale around."

But the gingernut cat said, "I suppose you realize that you'd have to pull down your house to make room for a pool, and then where would Mr A. watch TV?"

"That *would* be a problem," agreed Mrs Arbuckle.

So they said goodbye to the whale – and flew to Ethiopia to see an aardvark.

"I've always wanted to own my own aardvark," said Mrs Arbuckle.

The aardvark was waiting for them on a grassy slope. He was poking his tongue into an ants' nest and swallowing ants by the hundred.

"I heard you coming," said the aardvark. "I can hear things happening far away. I could listen for Mr A. coming home from the football and tell you when to put the dinner on."

"That would be handy," said Mrs Arbuckle.

"Well, I, for *one*," said the gingernut cat, "am not going to spend my days finding ants to feed an aardvark. Are *you* going to spend *your* days finding ants to feed an aardvark?"

"Maybe not," said Mrs Arbuckle.

So they said goodbye to the aardvark – and went up the Amazon to inverview a sloth.

99

"He's not here yet," said Mrs Arbuckle, looking all around.

"I *am* here," called the sloth. "Up here!"

"Will you come down or shall we come up?" asked Mrs Arbuckle.

"You come up," said the sloth. "I'm clumsy on the ground."

Mrs Arbuckle climbed up the rubber-tree.

"I'd be a pet with a difference," said the sloth. "You'd get to like me."

"I'm sure I should," agreed Mrs Arbuckle. "There's something about your face."

But the gingernut cat said, "You're out of your mind. What would the neighbours think if they called in for coffee and found you upside-down in the gum-tree?"

"They'd think I was dotty," said Mrs Arbuckle.

So they said goodbye to the sloth – and went to England to interview a frog.

The frog was waiting patiently in a puddle, looking all around with his big bright eyes.

"I have a most unusual voice," said the frog. "You could lie in bed at night and listen to me croak."

The frog puffed up his throat and made a really remarkable noise.

"Goodness!" said Mrs Arbuckle. "That would make a change from listening to the radio."

But the gingernut cat said, "Nonsense! Pets and people should sleep at night and make their noises in the daytime."

"I suppose they should," sighed Mrs Arbuckle.

So they said goodbye to the frog – and went to Canada to meet a grizzly bear.

"Well, here I am," said the grizzly bear. "You'll never find a furrier pet than me."

The grizzly bear looked at Mrs Arbuckle and Mrs Arbuckle looked at the grizzly bear.

"I like your little beady eyes," said Mrs Arbuckle.

But the gingernut cat said, "Take it from me – bear hugs can be very nasty in hot weather."

"Maybe so," said Mrs Arbuckle.

So they said goodbye to the grizzly bear – and went to Venezuela to talk to a toucan.

The toucan was gathering fruit in her great big beak, but she swallowed neatly before she spoke.

"I can carry a lot of fruit in my beak. You could send me to the shops for peaches or pears or plums or paw-paws . . ."

"That *would* be a help," said Mrs Arbuckle, "when Mr A. fancies fruit salad for his tea."

"But just suppose," said the gingernut cat, "that she tripped over a cat and swallowed the lot! Then there'd be no fruit salad for tea."

"Mr A. *would* be upset," sighed Mrs Arbuckle.

So they said goodbye to the toucan – and went to Tasmania to meet an echidna.

The echidna was having a sleep while he waited, rolled up in a prickly ball.

Mrs Arbuckle poked him gently between the spikes. He woke up and said, "Watch what you're doing!" Then he explained, "I doze a lot in the winter, you know. But in summer I'm a ball of energy. If you want any digging done *I'm* the pet for you."

The echidna started to dig. Soil flew up all around him, and in two minutes he had disappeared into the ground.

"That's a good trick!" cried Mrs Arbuckle.

But the gingernut cat said, "Who wants holes all over the garden? Does Mr A. want holes all over the garden?"

"Not really," replied Mrs Arbuckle.

So they said goodbye to the hole in the ground – and went to Japan to interview a butterfly.

"I'm a little late," said the butterfly. "It took me a while to get out of my cocoon."

He spread his wings in the sunlight.

"I'd be the loveliest pet for miles around," said the butterfly. "And what's more, you wouldn't have time to get tired of me. I only live for a couple of days."

"I've *always* loved purple," said Mrs Arbuckle.

"Wouldn't do at all," snapped the gingernut cat. "A pet

should go on and on, day after day. A pet should have regular meals, and sleep in the same old corner night after night. A pet should be something you can stroke."

"You're so right," sighed Mrs Arbuckle, "as always."

She was sad because there were no more applications.

So Mrs Arbuckle and the gingernut cat went home.

Mrs Emmeline Arbuckle made herself a cup of tea. The gingernut cat had a saucer of milk.

"How did it go?" asked Mr A.

"No good at all," replied Mrs Arbuckle. "Not one of the applicants was suitable."

"What a pity," said Mr A., and went on watching the football on TV.

"And now I suppose you'll be going home," said Mrs Arbuckle to the gingernut cat.

"I don't have a home. And I don't have prickles, or dig holes. I don't eat trees, or ants, or paw-paws, or hang upside-down, or need a pool to swim in. And I'm small and soft and *very* smart."

"Will *you* be my pet?" asked Mrs Arbuckle.

"Yes, yes, yes," said the gingernut cat. "I thought you'd *never* ask."

103

THE AMAZING PET

Marjorie Newman

Everyone in Robert's family was amazingly good at something – except Robert.

Robert's older brother, John, was amazingly clever. He had made a robot. It could move about, and pick things up.

"Amazing!" said everyone, when they looked at John and his robot.

Robert's older sister, Melanie, was amazingly good at acting. When she was in a play, lots of people came to watch her.

"Amazing!" they said. And they clapped and clapped.

Robert's younger brother, Clive, was amazingly good at painting and drawing.

Clive's pictures were always chosen to be pinned up on the wall at school. He'd had some pictures on television, as well.

"Amazing!" said everyone, when they looked at Clive and his pictures.

Robert couldn't paint. All his colours got mixed up. No one could tell what his pictures were meant to be. He couldn't even paint patterns.

Robert couldn't act. He didn't *want* to act very much. But he would have liked to be the horse in the school pantomime at Christmas.

Robert wasn't very clever. He couldn't make robots that walked about. He didn't know much about maths, or electronics.

It was nice for the others to be amazingly good at something. Robert could see that.

But he wished *he* was amazing too.

He told his mum.

"You're amazing enough for me!" she said. And she kissed him. She was looking at some photographs. She'd taken them herself. They were amazingly good. They were going to be printed in a newspaper.

Robert sighed.

He went into the garden. Dad was in the garden, looking at the roses. He told Dad.

"Mind where you're walking!" cried Dad. "You're amazing, all right! It's amazing how you can keep trampling over my flower-beds, without seeing them!"

Dad was cross, because his plants weren't growing as well as the man next door's. Dad's plants always won prizes in shows.

Robert sighed again. He went indoors. He went up to his bedroom, and sat on his bed. He thought hard. If only he could find something *he* could be amazingly good at . . .

Mush, the family cat, walked into the room. When she saw Robert, she stood still. Her tail was swishing. Her amber eyes were bright. Mush knew she wasn't allowed in the bedrooms; but she always went in, if she found a door open.

She jumped up on to Robert's lap. Robert stroked her. She settled down. Cats liked Robert, and he liked cats.

That was it! Robert sat up straight. He'd had a thought!

Animals liked him; and he liked animals. He wasn't amazing himself, but he would have an amazing pet!

Not a cat. Cats were ordinary. Not a dog, either. Nor a gerbil. Nor a rabbit. Nor a budgie. Nor a goldfish. Nor a tortoise.

Not even a grass snake. Or a lizard. Or tadpoles. Or a worm. Or a beetle.

Not a horse. Nor a donkey. Nor a goat. Nor a pig. Nor a sheep. Nor a cow.

They were farm animals. What about Zoo animals? What about the animals at the Wild Life Park near his home?

Robert fidgeted about while he thought. Mush was cross. He stepped off Robert's lap, and walked away. Robert didn't notice. He was thinking about deer, zebras, lions, hippos, giraffes . . .

Giraffes! A giraffe! That was IT! He would have a giraffe. He'd never heard of anyone who had a giraffe for a pet!

When Robert had visited the Wild Life Park, the giraffes had been his favourites. Seeing them had made him forget about Mr Huskey. Mr Huskey was the Park's director; and he was cross and fierce. He often shouted at children who visited the Park. He told them not to feed the animals.

But Robert had forgotten all about him when he saw the giraffes' soft, dark eyes; and their amazing long necks. The giraffe was amazing itself. And it would certainly make an amazing pet.

Robert jumped up. He went bouncing down the stairs.

"Mum! Mum!" he cried.

Then he stopped. He stood still. He remembered the fuss there had been when he'd wanted a pet rabbit. They'd said he wouldn't take care of it. They'd asked him if he had a hutch for it. They'd asked him how he would pay for its food.

In the end, he hadn't had a rabbit at all. This time, he would do things differently.

Robert walked down the rest of the stairs. He was thinking. This time, he'd find everything out *first*. He'd get everything ready. Then he'd tell them about the giraffe.

"Robert?"

Mum had heard him calling. She came out into the passage. "What's the matter?" she asked.

"Nothing," said Robert.

"He gets odder every day," said John. John was on his way to the shed, to alter his robot. Robert made a face at him. Then he thought about sheds.

"Mum," said Robert. "Can I have a shed? A very high shed?"

"Of course not!" said Mum. "We've got one shed already."

"But our shed's full up," said Robert. "It's full of Dad's tools, and the bikes, and John's workbench, and some of your photograph things. There's no space left!"

"What do you want space for?" asked Mum. Robert hesitated. But it was too soon to tell her a giraffe might need it for a house.

"Just – something," he said.

"Would the tent do?" asked Mum.

Robert smiled. "It might," he said. He could probably make a shelter with it.

He followed Mum into the room. He was still thinking. He could hang the tent material between the branch of the tree in the next door garden, and their own shed roof. The giraffe could go under there at night.

"Mum," he said, "do giraffes lie down when they go to sleep?"

"I don't know!" said Mum. "I've never thought about it. Look in a book, next time you go to the library. See if you can find out."

"Yes, I will," nodded Robert. A book about giraffes was a good idea. He could find out a lot about them, and still keep his secret.

Melanie went with him to the library. She went off to look for books about acting. Robert looked at the books about animals. He found some with giraffes in them. He piled up the books, and took them over to a table. Then he pulled up a chair, and settled himself to read.

"Giraffes are the tallest animals in the world!" he read. "They have long necks. They eat leaves from the tops of trees." Robert knew that. But he didn't know they had long tongues, as well. He imagined his giraffe pulling leaves off the branches of the trees in the next door garden. The man next door might not like that.

Robert would have to find out if he could give it other things to eat.

"Giraffes are camouflaged by their colouring," he read.

Good. Dad might not notice his giraffe, amongst the bushes at the bottom of the garden. It might not show up.

It would be a good thing, if Dad *didn't* notice. Dad would be sure to start worrying about the giraffe treading on his flower-beds. Only he needn't worry; because Robert would train it to keep on the paths.

"Giraffes hardly ever make a sound," he read. That was a good thing, too. People kept complaining about the dogs down the road because they barked. But giraffes were quiet.

Robert looked at the beautiful picture of a giraffe. His giraffe would look just like that. Beautiful.

It would need a name. Robert wanted to call it Beauty. But his family would probably laugh. He would call his giraffe George.

"Giraffes can run at about thirty miles per hour," said the book. Robert knew exactly how fast that was. He'd seen it on the speedometer of the car.

He'd take his giraffe out for walks. And when they got to the main road, he'd climb on to George's back. And off they'd go, to the sea-side!

"Giraffes have a little hairy brush on the end of their tails," he read. "They flick away flies with it."

"Flick away flies!" Robert liked the sound of those words. He wondered for a moment if he could dip the tail into paint, and hold up a big piece of paper. When George flicked *his* tail, it would paint patterns all over the paper. That would be as amazing as Clive's painting.

Robert looked up from his books. Melanie was sitting on the floor with her back against the bookshelves. She was reading a book about stage costumes.

Next Christmas, when the school had a pantomime, they wouldn't need a dressed-up horse. Robert would lead George on to the stage. He'd train George to do anything they wanted. At the end, George would bend his neck down, and look at the audience. And everyone would clap and clap . . . A pantomime giraffe. Amazing!

Robert closed his books and put them back on the shelves.

"I'm ready," he told Melanie.

She stood up, her eyes still on the book.

"Bring those for me," she said. Robert didn't see why he should. But he picked up the books she'd chosen, and took them to the desk for her. The librarian stamped them with the date and smiled at Robert.

"I've been finding out about giraffes," Robert told her. Then he noticed Melanie listening, so he was quiet.

But at home, at tea-time, Melanie said, "Robert, why did you want to find out about giraffes?"

Everyone stopped talking, or eating, and looked at him. Robert felt his face going red.

"I just wanted to know about them," he said.

"And a good thing too," said Mum. "Why shouldn't he be interested in giraffes?"

"He ought to go and ask Mr Huskey!" laughed John, teasing. Robert felt afraid, even thinking of it. The family all began to talk at once.

Melanie spluttered into her teacup.

Clive said, "Not Mr Huskey! He'd never dare! I know *I* wouldn't!"

Robert said, "Shut up about giraffes!"

And Mum said, "Robert!"

And Robert said, "Well!" And he got red, and cross. And Melanie started to talk about something else.

Robert thought about Mr Huskey. Mr Huskey was very fierce. And he didn't like children. But he would know a lot about giraffes. Mr Huskey could tell him how to look after George properly. Mr Huskey would know where to get a giraffe; and how much they cost.

Robert went hot all over. This was the first time he'd even wondered how much it would cost to buy a giraffe. Still, it would soon be his birthday. He had lots of aunts and uncles. He would ask if they could give him money, instead of a present. Just this once.

"Robert, it's your turn to clear the table," Clive said.

Robert didn't argue. He cleared the table quickly. Clive and Melanie were washing up. Everyone was busy.

"Mum, can I go out for a little while?" he asked.

"Be back before dark," she said. "And take care you don't get run over!"

She always said that. He always did take care. She usually said, "And don't go in any lonely places!"

She could have said that, too. The Wild Life Park wasn't a lonely place. And it closed before dark.

His legs began to shake, even before he reached the ticket-office at the gates. His voice sounded squeaky when he spoke to the ticket man.

"I want to speak to Mr Huskey, please," he said.

"Oh do you!" said the ticket man, peering down over his counter at Robert. "Mr Huskey is a very busy man! Why do you want him?"

Robert swallowed hard. He knew his face was bright red. He was afraid the man was going to say no, without even asking Mr Huskey.

"It's — it's about the animals," he said. "And it's very, very important."

And then Mr Huskey himself came out from the office behind the ticket man.

"What's all this?" he demanded.

His voice was loud and angry.

"I'd like to ask you about – giraffes," said Robert. "Please!"

He nearly ran away, without waiting for Mr Huskey to answer. Then he thought about George.

"I've been to the library," he said. "But the books didn't tell me how to feed giraffes. Or if they sleep lying down." He took a breath. Then he went on. "And they didn't say how much it costs to buy a giraffe."

He stopped talking. He didn't dare to look up.

"You like giraffes, do you?" said Mr Huskey. He'd stopped shouting.

"Oh yes! I want a giraffe for a pet!" said Robert; and it was quite easy to look up. The ticket man was laughing. It was the way John laughed. Robert turned away, to go home. But Mr Huskey said, "Hey! Do you want to know, or not?"

Robert turned back. "Yes," he said, "I do!"

"Come on," said Mr Huskey. "Let's go and see my giraffes."

Robert went with Mr Huskey to the enclosure. He looked at

112

the three giraffes. They were big. Very big. He'd forgotten *how* big.

"Do they lie down to sleep?" he asked.

"Giraffes don't sleep much at all," said Mr Huskey. "When they do, they lie down like a cow does. And they often rest their heads round on their backs."

"Oh," said Robert. "Do they eat leaves?" he asked.

"Yes, we give them branches from hazel trees, and oak trees," said Mr Huskey. "We give them hay, as well. And a type of dairy-nuts, oats and bran."

"Oh," said Robert again. It sounded expensive.

"They are very nervous animals," Mr Huskey said. "We have to keep them very quiet. If they get frightened, they might die."

"Oh," said Robert. He imagined George on the main road, with the cars pelting by. He imagined George on the hot, brightly lit stage. He imagined George being shouted at by Dad and the man next door.

Mr Huskey put a hand on Robert's shoulder.

"What about adopting a giraffe?" he said. "You could choose one of these. It could be like your own – only you could leave it here where it's happy. You could come and visit it whenever you want to."

Robert thought about this. But he shook his head. He could never feel that a giraffe who lived in a Wild Life Park was his own pet.

"No thank you," he said.

Together, he and Mr Huskey walked back to the entrance gates. When they reached them, Mr Huskey said, "Wait a moment!"

Robert waited, drearily kicking his toe against the doorstep.

"Where's your giraffe, then?" asked the ticket man. He was grinning. Robert hated him.

Mr Huskey came back, with a large white envelope. He gave it to Robert.

"There," he said. "There's a free pass inside that envelope. Come in and visit the animals whenever you like!"

The ticket man stopped grinning. Robert looked at the free pass, then at Mr Huskey.

"Thank you very much," he said. And he felt a little better.

He walked home slowly, and went indoors. The family was in the sitting room.

Robert sat down quietly.

"What's in the envelope, Rob?" asked Dad.

"A free pass to the Wild Life Park," said Robert.

"WHAT?" cried everyone. "Where did you get it?"

Robert told them. When he said he'd wanted a giraffe for a pet, everyone laughed; so he didn't tell them why he'd wanted it.

But when he said he'd been to the Park, and asked Mr Huskey how to take care of giraffes, everyone was very quiet. They all looked at him with their mouths open.

"Did you really go and talk to Mr Huskey?" said John, at last.

"Yes," said Robert. "He's a nice man, when you get to know him."

"You are AMAZING!" said Dad.

Robert sat up straight. *He* was amazing?

"Yes, you are!" cried Mum, and John, and Melanie, and Clive. "You are amazingly brave!"

Robert looked at them all. And he began to grin. He was amazing! Just like the rest of them!

THE GREAT HAMSTER HUNT

Lenore and Erik Blegvad

Nicholas wanted a hamster.

Mother said no to that.

"But Tony has a hamster," Nicholas said.

"Oh?" said Mother. "Then go next door and look at his."

"I don't think your mother likes little furry creatures," Father remarked.

"Well, Tony's mother doesn't either," Nicholas told him. "And *they* have one."

Mother sighed. "Then Tony's mother is just nicer than I am," she added. "Right?"

"I suppose so," said Nicholas sadly.

One day Tony came to the door.

"We're going away for a week," he said to Nicholas's mother. "Do you think Nicholas would take care of my hamster for me if I asked him nicely?"

Nicholas jumped up from his chair.

"You don't have to ask me nicely," he shouted. "The answer is *yes!*"

So Tony's hamster came to stay with Nicholas for a week. Its name was Harvey. It lived in a shiny cage with wire on top and a front sliding wall of glass. There was also a wheel that went around and around when Harvey ran inside it. On the side of the cage was a water bottle with a tube for Harvey to drink from.

Before Tony left, he told Nicholas how to take care of Harvey.

"You have to change the cedar shavings in the cage every few days," he said. He had brought a bag of them with him. He had also brought a bag of special hamster food, which was made up of fourteen different kinds of seeds and nuts. "You can give him lettuce or carrot tops, too," Tony said. "But never, never give him any meat."

"Why not?" Nicholas asked.

Tony explained that, if hamsters were fed meat, they would get to like the taste of it so much they would try to eat each other when there was more than one hamster in a cage.

"That's called being 'carnivorous' or 'flesh eating'," Tony said. "A hamster should stay 'herbivorous', which is 'plant eating'."

"Oh," said Nicholas. "Wow!" He would be very careful not

116

to give Harvey any meat. "Can I take him out of his cage?" he asked as Tony was leaving.

"Yes," Tony said. "But watch out he doesn't disappear. Good-bye." Then, halfway across the garden, he called, "Hey, I forgot to tell you. Hamsters are nocturnal, in case you didn't know. 'Bye."

"What's that mean?" Nicholas called back. But Tony had already gone.

All that week Nicholas took good care of Harvey. He fed him and played with him and cleaned his cage carefully. But he always remembered that Harvey was Tony's hamster. He would hold it in his hand, feeling its little cold feet on his palm and its warm, quivering fur, and he would whisper, "Oh, I wish I had a hamster just like you!"

Harvey seemed to sleep most of the day, but at night he loved to run around and around inside his exercise wheel.

Nicholas loved the squeaky noise of Harvey's wheel. It put him to sleep at night just like a lullaby.

"Yes, I wish I had a hamster just like Harvey," Nicholas said sadly to himself.

All too soon the week was up. Tony would be coming home the next evening. After supper Nicholas decided to clean Harvey's cage for the last time. He took it down to the kitchen. First he put Harvey in a large carton, where he could watch him. Then, very carefully, he slid out the glass panel from the cage, and very carefully he started to put the glass on the kitchen table, but all of a sudden . . .

CRASH!

The glass slipped from his hands and broke into a million pieces all over the kitchen floor!

Nicholas's father helped to sweep them up.

"We'll have to find some way of keeping Harvey in his cage until we can buy another piece of glass tomorrow morning," he said.

He found a piece of heavy cardboard, cut it to the right size, and slid it into the place where the glass had been. It worked very well.

When they had finished, it was time for Nicholas to go to bed. He was very sad because it was Harvey's last night in his house. He let Harvey play outside the cage for a longer time than usual. At last he put him in the cage and looked at him through the wires on top.

"Good night, Harvey," he whispered. "We did have a good time, didn't we?" Then he turned out his light and soon fell asleep to the sound of the squeaking exercise wheel.

When morning came, Nicholas woke up early to have as much time as possible with Harvey before Tony came back. He looked in through the top of the cage to say, "Good morning," but . . . would you believe it? *The cage was empty!*

"Oh, no!" Mother said when she heard.

"Ho ho," Father said when he went to see. 'He's chewed a hole right through the cardboard. We are going to have a grand time finding him!"

So they began to look – right then, before breafast.

They looked under Nicholas's bed. They looked in his dresser drawers. They looked in his cupboard and in all the boxes in the cupboard and in all the pockets of all the clothes in the cupboard. They looked in the toy soldier box and behind the curtains and under Nicholas's pillow and in between his blankets and inside his gramophone and even in his slippers.

When they had not found a trace of Harvey, Father sat down on Nicholas's bed.

"He could be anywhere, you know," he said gloomily. "Not just here in your room."

"And we'll never find him before Tony comes back," Nicholas said, and looked as though he might cry.

"What *are* we going to do?" Mother asked.

All at once, Father seemed to have the answer.

"We must go on a hunt for him," he said firmly. "As if he were a lion. Or an elephant. We must bring him back alive! And to do that, we must trap him." He jumped up. "First," he continued, "I'll need lots of plastic wastebaskets," and he looked at Mother.

"There's that little one in the bathroom," Mother said helpfully.

"No, no," Father said. "We must have lots more." And he dressed very quickly and rushed out of the house.

While he was gone, Nicholas and his mother continued to look for Harvey. They were still looking when Father came back with eight plastic wastebaskets. He also brought a new piece of glass for Harvey's cage.

"I borrowed the wastebaskets from the owner of the iron-mongers," he explained. "He was very interested in my plan."

"I can imagine," Mother said. "So am I. What is it?"

But Father was too busy to answer. He put a small pile of books in the middle of each room in the house and leaned a wastebasket against each pile so that the baskets were half lying, half standing.

'Now," he said, "I need blocks, long wooden blocks, Nicholas. And towels," he said to Mother. "Plenty of towels. And don't forget the lettuce."

"No," said Mother. "How could I forget the lettuce?"

So Father took the blocks and the towels and the lettuce and he made . . .

Hamster traps!

This is a hamster trap.

"Now, all we have to do is to wait for Harvey to eat his way up the ramp and fall into one of the wastebaskets," Father explained. "The plastic is too slippery for him to climb out." And he started to read his morning paper.

Mother looked at Nicholas.

"Do you think . . .?" Nicholas began.

"Not really," Mother said, and picked up her purse. "We'd better take a little shopping trip, just in case."

Mother took Nicholas to the pet store.

"We need a hamster, please," she said. "White, with pink eyes and a pink nose. About four inches long."

"I'm sorry," the pet store owner said. "We have only brown hamsters at the moment. Will they do?"

"No, no," Mother said. "They won't do at all. Thank you. We'll have to try somewhere else."

And they did. They tried many other places until quite late in the afternoon.

Mother telephoned Father from the next town where she and Nicholas had finally gone on their search.

"Father hasn't caught anything," she reported to Nicholas.

"And we haven't found another white hamster for Tony," Nicholas said, again feeling as if he might cry. "Now we'll have to buy him a brown one that won't even look like Harvey."

But when they got to the last pet shop, they were delighted to see a hamster that looked very much like Harvey. It was white with pink eyes and a pink nose, and it was just about four inches long, if you did not count its extra-long whiskers.

"That's the one," Mother said, and took out her purse. The shopkeeper put the hamster in a little cardboard box with air holes punched in top. Nicholas held it carefully on his lap on the way home. He felt much better now. At least Tony would have a hamster that could remind him of Harvey.

When they got home, Nicholas put the new hamster in Harvey's cage, which they'd taken to the kitchen. It ran around in Harvey's treadmill a few times. Then it curled up in a corner of the cage and went to sleep.

"I hope Tony will get to like you as much as he liked Harvey," Nicholas said to it. "Anyway, I like you. I wish you were my hamster."

"And I wish those traps had worked," Father said, looking at his wastebaskets. "I can't understand what went wrong." He picked up the now wilted lettuce leaves and threw them away. Nicholas put the blocks back in his room. Mother folded up the towels again.

121

"I don't know about you," she said, turning on the lamps in the living room, "but I'm exhausted. I am going to play myself some relaxing music." She sat down at the piano and turned the pages of her music book.

"A nocturne would do it," Father said, settling down to listen. Nicholas turned his head.

"A what?" he asked. Where had he heard that word before?

"A nocturne is a piece of night music, dreamy, cloudy kind of music. The word 'nocturne' has to do with night."

"Then that's what Tony meant," Nicholas cried, jumping up. "And that's why Harvey sleeps all day and plays all night. All hamsters do. They're nocturnal!"

He rushed into the dark kitchen, where, sure enough, the new hamster had awakened and was running furiously around Harvey's exercise wheel, just as Harvey used to do at night.

"Now is the time to look for Harvey," Nicholas shouted, running up the stairs to his room. He tiptoed over to his bed and sat down in the dark. Everything was very quiet. Then downstairs his mother started playing the nocturne – very softly. It sounded very nocturnal indeed. Nicholas listened, but he was also listening for something else – for the sound of a hamster waking up to play. What kind of sound would that be?

Then he heard it. A rustle and a scratch. And another rustle and another scratch! It came from underneath his bookshelf! Nicholas turned on his lamp, just in time to see Harvey's pink nose poking out from the tiniest crack between the bookshelf and the wall!

Nicholas waited until Harvey had squeezed himself out into the room, and then he swooped down and picked him up.

"I've got him!" he called to his parents, and ran downstairs.

"Good for you," Father said. "That's the way to hunt hamsters!"

"I never thought I'd consider a hamster so absolutely beautiful," said Mother, patting the top of Harvey's head with one finger. "How did you like my hamster music, Harvey?"

Then Nicholas put Harvey back in his cage. The two hamsters

stared at each other for a moment. Then the new hamster returned to the exercise wheel and Harvey began to eat.

Nicholas and his parents watched them, and Nicholas began to feel a strange feeling of wildest hope. He looked at his mother and father. Did he dare to ask?

"Do you think . . ." he began, ". . . if I took very good care of him . . . that maybe . . .?" His mother and father nodded, almost together.

"Yes," his father said. "You're an expert on hamsters. I don't see why you shouldn't have one of your own."

"Yes," agreed Nicholas's mother. "I rather like hamsters now. We'll get him a cage in the morning. Tonight he can sleep in a plastic wastebasket."

Just then the doorbell rang. It was Tony. He had come to fetch Harvey. He was very surprised to see another white hamster in Harvey's cage. Nicholas took his new hamster out, and it ran up his arm to sit on his shoulder.

"Hey," Tony said. "How come you've got a hamster? It's not your birthday or anything, is it?"

Nicholas shook his head. "No," he said happily. "It was just by accident."

Tony was puzzled. "Oh," was all he said, as if he understood. But he didn't. He picked up Harvey's cage and the bags of food and shavings. "Well, thanks a lot for taking care of Harvey for me."

Nicholas went with him to the door. "You're welcome," he said. "See you tomorrow."

In the mirror next to the front door, Nicholas saw himself with his hamster. The hamster was sitting on Nicholas's head. It looked very happy up there, and underneath it Nicholas looked happy, too.

WOL HELPS OUT

Farley Mowat

When Farley Mowat was growing up in Saskatchewan, Canada, he and his schoolmate, Bruce, were encouraged by their natural-science teacher to hunt for the nest of great horned owls. Out of this searching, Farley gained a pet owlet that became the enormous and intrepid Wol (the name of the owl in A. A. Milne's Pooh stories) and a timid owl whom he called Weeps. Mutt was his black-and-white almost-setter.

The banks of the Saskatchewan River were very steep where the river ran through the prairie to the south of Saskatoon; and about two miles downstream from the city was a perfect place for digging caves. Bruce and Murray and I had our summer headquarters down there, in an old cave some hobos had dug a long time ago. They had fixed it up with logs and pieces of wood so it wouldn't collapse. You have to be careful of caves, because if they don't have good strong logs to hold up the roof, the whole thing can fall down and kill you. This was a good cave we had, though; my Dad had even come there and looked it over to make sure it was safe for us.

It had a door made of a piece of tin-roofing, and there was a smoke-stack going up through the ceiling. Inside was a sort of bench where you could lie down, and we had two old butter-tubs for chairs. We put dry hay down on the floor for a carpet, and under the hay was a secret hole where we could hide anything that was specially valuable.

The river ran only a hop-skip-and-a-jump from the door of the cave. There was a big sand bar close by which made a backwater where the current was slow enough for swimming. Standing right beside the swimming hole was the biggest cottonwood tree in the whole of Saskatchewan. One of its branches stuck straight out over the water, and there were old marks on it where a rope had cut into the bark. An Indian who was being chased by the Mounties, a long, long time ago, was supposed to have hanged himself on that branch so the Mounties wouldn't catch him alive.

We used to go to our cave a couple of times a week during the summer holidays, and usually we took the owls along. Wol had learned how to ride on the handle-bars of my bicycle; but Weeps couldn't keep his balance there, so we built a kind of box for him and tied it to the carrier behind the seat. Mutt and Rex used to come, too, chasing cows whenever they got a chance, or racing away across the prairie after jack rabbits.

We would bike out to the end of Third Avenue and then along an old Indian trail which ran along the top of the riverbank. When we got close to the cave we would hide our bikes in the willows and then climb down the bank and follow a secret path. There were some pretty tough kids in Saskatoon, and we didn't want them to find our cave if we could help it.

Wol loved those trips. All the way out he would bounce up and down on the handle-bars, hooting to himself with excitement, or hooting out insults at any passing dog. When we came to the place where we hid the bikes, he would fly up into the poplars and follow us through the tops of the trees. He usually stayed pretty close, though; because, if he didn't, some crows would be sure to spot him and then they would call up all the other crows for miles around and try to mob him. When that happened, he would come zooming down to the cave and bang on the door with his beak until we let him in. He wasn't afraid of the crows; it was just that he couldn't fight back when they tormented him. As for Weeps, he usually stayed right in the cave, where he felt safe.

One summer afternoon, when we were at the cave, we

decided to go for a swim. The three of us shucked off our clothes and raced for the sand bar, hollering at each other: "Last one in's a Dutchman!"

In half a minute we were in the water, splashing around and rolling in the slippery black mud along the edge of the sand bar. It was great stuff to fight with. Nice and soft and slithery, it packed into mushy mud-balls that made a wonderful splash when they hit something.

Whenever we went swimming, Wol would come along and find a perch in the Hanging Tree where he could watch the fun. He would get out on the big limb that hung over the water, and the more fuss and noise we made, the more excited he became. He would walk back and forth along the limb, *hoo-hooing* and ruffling his feathers, and you could tell he felt he was missing out on the fun.

This particular day he couldn't stand it any longer, so he came down out of the tree and waddled right to the river's edge.

We were skylarking on the sand bar when I saw him, so I

127

gave out a yell: "Hey, Wol! C'mon there, Wol, old owl! C'mon out here!"

Of course I thought he would fly across the strip of open water and light on the dry sand where we were playing. But I forgot Wol had never had any experience with water before, except in his drinking bowl at home.

He got his experience in a hurry. Instead of spreading his wings, he lifted up one foot very deliberately and started to walk across the water toward us.

It didn't take him long to find out he couldn't do it. There was an almighty splash, and spray flew every which way. By the time we raced across and fished him out, he was half-drowned and about the sickest bird you ever saw. His feathers were plastered down until he looked as skinny as a plucked chicken. The slimy black mud hadn't improved his looks much, either.

I carried him ashore, but he didn't thank me for it. His feelings were hurt worse than he was, and after he had shaken most of the water out of his feathers, he went gallumphing off through the woods towards home, on foot (he was too wet to fly), without a backward glance.

Towards the middle of July, Bruce and I got permission from our parents to spend a night in the cave. Murray couldn't come because his mother wouldn't let him. We took Wol and Weeps with us, and of course we had both dogs.

In the afternoon we went for a hike over the prairie, looking for birds. Mutt, who was running ahead of us, flushed a prairie chicken off her nest. There were ten eggs in the nest, and they were just hatching out.

We sat down beside the nest and watched. In an hour's time, seven of the little chickens had hatched before our eyes. It was pretty exciting to see, and Wol seemed just as curious about it as we were. Then all of a sudden three of the newly hatched little birds slipped out of the nest and scuttled straight for Wol. Before he could move they were underneath him, crowding against his big feet, and *peep-peeping* happily. I guess they thought he was their mother, because they hadn't seen their real mother yet.

Wol was so surprised he didn't know what to do. He kept lifting up one foot and then the other to shake off the little ones. When the other four babies joined the first three, Wol began to get nervous. But finally he seemed to resign himself to being a mother, and he fluffed his feathers out and lowered himself very gently to the ground.

Bruce and I nearly died laughing. The sight of the baby prairie chickens popping their heads out through Wol's feathers, and that great big beak of his snapping anxiously in the air right over their heads, was the silliest thing I've ever seen. I guess Wol knew it was silly, too, but he couldn't figure how to get out of the mess he was in. He kept looking at me as if he were saying: "For Heaven's sake, DO something!"

I don't know how long he would have stayed there, but we began to worry that the real mother might not find her chicks, so I finally lifted him up and put him on my shoulder, and we went back to the cave for supper.

We'd had a good laugh at Wol, but he had the laugh on us before the day was done.

After we had eaten, we decided to go down to the riverbank

and wait for the sun to set. A pair of coyotes lived on the opposite bank of the river, and every evening just at sunset one of them would climb a little hill and sit there howling. It was a scary sound, but we liked it because it made us feel that this was the olden times, and the prairie belonged to us, to the buffaloes and the Indians, and to the prairie wolves.

Wol was sitting in the Hanging Tree, and Rex and Mutt had gone off somewhere on a hunting trip of their own. It was growing dusk when we heard a lot of crashing in the trees behind us. We turned around just as two big kids came into sight. They were two of the toughest kids in Saskatoon. If they hadn't come on us so suddenly, we would have been running before they ever saw us. But now it was too late to run – they would have caught us before we could go ten feet. The only thing we could do was sit where we were and hope they would leave us alone.

What a hope *that* was! They came right over and one of them reached down and grabbed Bruce and started to twist his arm behind his back.

"Listen, you little rats," he said, "we heard you got a cave someplace down here. You're too young to own a cave, so we're taking over. Show us where it is, or I'll twist your arm right off!"

The other big kid made a grab for me, but I slipped past him and was starting to run when he stuck his foot out and tripped me. Then he sat on me.

"Say, Joe," he said to his pal, "I got an idea. Either these kids tell us where the cave is, or we tie 'em to the Hanging Tree and leave 'em there all night with the Injun's ghost."

Just then the coyote across the river gave a howl. All four of us jumped a little, what with the talk of ghosts – but Joe said: "That ain't nothing. Just a coyote howling. You going to tell us, kid? Or do we tie you to the tree?"

Bruce and I knew they were only trying to scare us, but we were scared all right. I was just opening my mouth to tell them where the cave was when Wol took a hand in things.

He had been sitting on the big limb of the Hanging Tree and, since it was almost dark by then, he looked like a big white blob up there. I don't think he'd been paying much attention to what was happening on the ground below him, but when that coyote howled, he must have thought it was some kind of challenge. He opened his beak and gave the Owl Hunting Scream.

Did you ever hear a horned owl scream? Usually they do it at night to scare any mice or rabbits that happen to be hiding near into jumping or running. Then the owl swoops down and grabs them. If you've ever heard an owl scream, you'll know it's just about the most scary sound in all the world.

When Wol cut loose, it made even my skin creep – and I knew what it was; but the two big kids didn't know.

Their heads jerked up, and they saw the ghostly white shape that was Wol up there in the Hanging Tree. And then they were off and running. They went right through the poplar woods like a couple of charging buffaloes, and we could still hear them breaking brush when they were half a mile away. My guess is that they ran all the way to Saskatoon.

131

When they were out of hearing, Bruce stood up and began rubbing his arm. Then he looked at Wol.

"Boy!" he said. "You sure scared those two roughnecks silly! But did you have to scare *me* right out of my skin, too?"

"Hoo-HOO-hoo-hoo-hoo-HOO!" Wol chuckled as he floated down out of the tree and lit upon my shoulder.

LOB'S GIRL

Joan Aiken

Some people choose their dogs, and some dogs choose their people. The Pengelly family had no say in the choosing of Lob; he came to them in the second way, and very decisively.

It began on the beach, the summer when Sandy was five, Don, her older brother, twelve, and the twins were three. Sandy was really Alexandra, because her grandmother had a beautiful picture of a queen in a diamond tiara and high collar of pearls. It hung by Grandma Pearce's kitchen sink and was as familiar as the doormat. When Sandy was born everyone agreed that she was the living spit of the picture, and so she was called Alexandra, and Sandy for short.

On this summer day she was lying peacefully reading a comic and not keeping an eye on the twins who didn't need it because they were occupied in seeing which of them could wrap the most seaweed round the other one's legs. Father – Bert Pengelly – and Don were up on the Hard, painting the bottom boards of the boat in which Father went fishing for pilchards. And Mother – Jean Pengelly – was getting ahead with making the Christmas puddings because she never felt easy in her mind if they weren't made and safely put away by the end of August. As usual, each member of the family was happily getting on with its own affairs. Little did they guess how soon this state of things would be changed by the large new member who was going to erupt his way into their midst.

133

Sandy rolled on to her back to make sure that the twins were not climbing on slippery rocks or getting cut off by the tide. At the same moment a large body struck her forcibly in the midriff and she was covered by flying sand. Instinctively she shut her eyes, and felt the sand being wiped off her face by something that seemed like a warm, rough, damp flannel. She opened her eyes and looked. It was a tongue. Its owner was a large and bouncy young Alsatian, or German Shepherd, with topaz eyes, black-tipped prick ears, a thick soft coat, and a bushy black-tipped tail.

"Lob!" shouted a man farther up the beach. "Lob, come here!"

But Lob, as if trying to atone for the surprise he had given her, went on licking the sand off Sandy's face, wagging his tail so hard, meanwhile, that he kept on knocking up more clouds of sand. His owner, a grey-haired man with a limp, walked over as quickly as he could and seized the dog by the collar.

"I hope he didn't give you a fright?" the man said to Sandy. "He meant it in play – he's only young."

"Oh, no, I think he's *beautiful*," said Sandy truly. She picked up a bit of driftwood and threw it. Lob, whisking easily out of his master's grip, was after it like a sand-coloured bullet. He came back with the stick, beaming, and gave it to Sandy. At the same time he gave himself, though no one else was aware of this at the time. But with Sandy too it was love at first sight, and when, after a lot more stick-throwing, she and the twins joined Father and Don to go home for tea, they cast many a backward glance at Lob being led firmly away by his master.

"I wish we could play with him every day," sighed Tessa.

"Why can't we?" said Tim.

Sandy explained. "Because Mr Dodsworth, who owns him, is from Liverpool, and he is only staying at the Fisherman's Arms till Saturday."

"Is Liverpool a long way off?"

"Right at the other end of England from Cornwall, I'm afraid," said their father.

It was a Cornish fishing village where the Pengelly family

lived, with rocks and cliffs and a strip of beach and a little round harbour, and palm trees growing in the gardens of the little white-washed stone houses. The village was approached by a narrow, steep, twisting hill, and guarded by a notice that said: "Low gear for 1½ miles. Dangerous to Cyclists."

The Pengelly children went home to Cornish cream and jam, thinking they had seen the last of Lob. But they were much mistaken. The whole family was playing Beggar-my-Neighbour round the fire in the front room after supper when there was a loud thump and crash of china in the kitchen.

"My Christmas puddings!" exclaimed Jean, and ran out.

"Did you put dynamite in them?" her husband called.

But it was Lob, who, finding the front door shut, had gone round to the back and bounced in through the open kitchen window, where the puddings were cooling on the sill. Luckily only the smallest was knocked down and broken.

Lob stood on his hind legs and plastered Sandy's face with licks. Then he did the same for the twins, who shrieked with joy.

"Where did this friend of yours come from?" asked Bert Pengelly.

"He's staying at the Fisherman's Arms – I mean his owner is."

"Then he must go back there. Find a bit of string, Sandy, to tie to his collar."

"I wonder how he found his way here?" Mrs Pengelly said, when the reluctant Lob had been led whining away, and Sandy had explained about their afternoon's game on the beach. "Fisherman's Arms is right round the other side of the harbour."

Lob's owner scolded him and thanked Mr Pengelly for bringing him back. Jean Pengelly warned the children that they had better not encourage Lob any more if they met him on the beach, or it would only lead to more trouble. So they dutifully took no notice of him the next day – until he spoiled their good resolutions by dashing up to them with joyful barks, wagging his tail so hard that he winded Tess and knocked Tim's legs from under him.

They had a happy day, playing on the sand.

Next day was Saturday. Sandy had found out that Mr Dodsworth was to catch the half-past nine train. She went out secretly, down to the station, nodded to Mr Hoskins, the stationmaster, who wouldn't dream of charging any local for a platform ticket, and climbed up on the footbridge that led over the tracks. She didn't want to be seen, but she did want to see. She saw Mr Dodsworth get on the train, accompanied by an unhappy-looking Lob with drooping ears and tail. Then she saw the train slide away out of sight round the next headland, with a melancholy wail that sounded like Lob's last goodbye.

Sandy wished she hadn't had the idea of coming to the station. She walked home miserably, with her shoulders hunched and her hands in her pockets. For the rest of the day she was so cross and unlike herself that Tess and Tim were quite surprised, and her mother gave her a dose of senna.

A week passed. Then, one evening, Mrs Pengelly and the younger children were in the front room playing ludo. Mr Pengelly and Don had gone fishing on the evening tide. If your father is a fisherman he will never be home at the same time from one week to the next.

Suddenly, history repeating itself, there was a crash from the kitchen. Jean Pengelly leapt up, crying, "My blackberry jelly!" They had spent the morning picking and the afternoon boiling fruit.

But Sandy was ahead of her mother. With flushed cheeks and eyes like stars she had darted into the kitchen, where she and Lob were hugging one another in a frenzy of joy. About a yard of his tongue was out, and he was licking every part of her that he could reach.

"Good heavens!" exclaimed Jean. "How in the world did he get here?"

"He must have walked," said Sandy. "Look at his feet."

They were worn, dusty, and tarry. One had a cut on the pad.

"They ought to be bathed," said Jean Pengelly. "Sandy, run a bowl of warm water while I get the disinfectant."

"What'll we do about him, Mum?" asked Sandy anxiously.

Mrs Pengelly looked at her daughter's pleading eyes and sighed.

"He must go back to his owner of course," she said, making her voice firm. "Your dad can get the address from the Fisherman's tomorrow, and phone him or send a telegram. In the meantime he'd better have a long drink and a good meal."

Lob was very grateful for the drink and the meal, and made no objection to having his feet washed. Then he flopped down on the hearthrug and slept in front of the fire they had lit because it was a cold, wet evening, with his head on Sandy's feet. He was a very tired dog. He had walked all the way from Liverpool to Cornwall, which is more than four hundred miles.

Next day Mr Pengelly phoned Lob's owner, and the following morning Mr Dodsworth arrived off the train, decidedly put out, to take his pet home. That parting was worse than the first. Lob whined, Don walked out of the house, the twins burst out crying, and Sandy crept up to her bedroom afterwards and lay with her face pressed into the quilt, feeling as if she were bruised all over.

Jean Pengelly took them all into Plymouth to the circus next day and the twins cheered up a little, but even the hour's ride on the train each way and the Liberty horses and performing seals could not cure Sandy's sore heart.

She need not have bothered, though. In ten days' time Lob was back – limping this time, with a torn ear and a patch missing out of his furry coat, as if he had met and tangled with an enemy or two in the course of his four-hundred-mile walk.

Bert Pengelly rang up Liverpool again. Mr Dodsworth, when he answered, sounded weary. He said, "That dog has already cost me two days that I can't spare away from my work – plus endless time in police stations and drafting newspaper advertisements. I'm too old for these ups and downs. I think we'd better face the fact, Mr Pengelly, that it's your family he wants to stay with – that is, if you want to have him."

Bert Pengelly gulped. He was not a rich man; and Lob was a pedigree dog. He said cautiously, "How much would you be asking for him?"

"Good heavens, man, I'm not suggesting I'd *sell* him to you. You must have him as a gift. Think of the train fares I'll be saving. You'll be doing me a good turn."

"Is he a big eater?" Bert asked doubtfully.

By this time the children, breathless in the background listening to one side of this conversation, had realized what was in the wind and were dancing up and down with their hands clasped beseechingly.

"Oh, not for his size," Lob's owner assured Bert. "Two or three pounds of meat a day and some vegetables and gravy and biscuits – he does very well on that."

Alexandra's father looked over the telephone at his daughter's swimming eyes and trembling lips. He reached a decision. "Well then, Mr Dodsworth," he said briskly, "we'll accept your offer and thank you very much. The children will be overjoyed and you can be sure that Lob has come to a good home. They'll look after him and see he gets enough exercise. But I can tell you," he ended firmly, "if he wants to settle in with us he'll have to learn to eat a lot of fish."

So that was how Lob came to live with the Pengelly family. Everybody loved him and he loved them all. But there was never any question who came first with him. He was Sandy's dog. He slept by her bed, and followed her everywhere he was allowed.

Nine years went by, and each summer Mr Dodsworth came back to stay at the Fisherman's Arms and call on his erstwhile dog. Lob always met him with recognition and dignified pleasure, accompanied him for a walk or two – but showed no signs of wishing to return to Liverpool. His place, he intimated, was definitely with the Pengellys.

In the course of nine years Lob changed less than Sandy. As she went into her teens he became a little slower, a little stiffer, there was a touch of grey on his nose, but he was still a handsome dog. He and Sandy loved one another devotedly.

One evening in October all the summer visitors had left, and the little fishing town looked empty and secretive. It was a wet, windy dusk. When the children came home from school – even the twins were at high school now, and Don was a full-fledged fisherman – Jean Pengelly said, "Sandy, your Aunt Rebecca says she's lonesome because Uncle Will Hoskins has gone out trawling, and she wants one of you to go and spend the evening with her. You go, dear; you can take your homework with you."

Sandy looked far from enthusiastic.

"Can I take Lob with me?"

"You know Aunt Becky doesn't like dogs – Oh, very well," sighed Mrs Pengelly. "I suppose she'll have to put up with him as well as you."

Reluctantly Sandy tidied herself, took her school bag, put on the damp raincoat she had just taken off, fastened Lob's lead to his collar, and set off to walk through the dusk to Aunt Becky's cottage, which was five minutes' climb up the steep hill.

The wind was howling through the shrouds of boats down on the Hard.

"Put on some cheerful music, do," said Jean Pengelly to the nearest twin. "Anything to drown that wretched sound while I make your dad's supper." So Don, who had just come in, put on some rock music, loud. Which was why the Pengellys did not hear the truck hurtle down the hill and crash against the post office wall a few minutes later.

Dr Travers was driving through Cornwall with his wife, taking a late holiday before patients began coming down with winter colds and 'flu. He saw the sign that said, "Steep Hill. Low gear for 1½ miles." Dutifully he changed down.

"We must be nearly there," said his wife, looking out of her window. "I noticed a sign that said the Fisherman's Arms was two miles. What a narrow, dangerous hill! But the cottages are pretty – Oh, Frank, stop, *stop*! There's a child, I'm sure it's a child – by the wall there!"

Dr Travers jammed on his brakes and brought the car to a

stop. A little stream ran down by the road in a shallow stone culvert, and half in the water lay something that looked, in the dusk, like a pile of clothes – or was it the body of a child? Mrs Travers was out of the car in a flash, but her husband was quicker.

"Don't touch her, Emily!" he said sharply. "She's been hit. Can't be more than a few minutes. Remember that truck that overtook us half a mile back, speeding like the devil? Here, quick, go into that house and phone for an ambulance. The girl's in a bad way. I'll stay here and do what I can to stop the bleeding. Don't waste a minute."

Doctors are expert at stopping dangerous bleeding, for they know the right places to press. This Dr Travers was able to do, but he didn't dare do more; the girl was lying in a queerly crumpled heap and he guessed she had a number of bones broken, that it would be highly dangerous to move her. He watched her with great concentration, wondering where the truck had got to, and what other damage it had done.

Mrs Travers was very quick. She had seen plenty of accident cases and knew the importance of speed. The first cottage she tried had a phone; in four minutes she was back, and in six an ambulance was wailing down the hill.

Its attendants lifted the child on to a stretcher as carefully as if she were made of fine thistledown. The ambulance sped off to Plymouth – for the local cottage hospital did not take serious accident cases – and Dr Travers went down to the police station to report what he had done.

He found that the police already knew about the speeding truck – which had suffered from brake-fade and ended up with its radiator halfway through the post office wall. The driver was concussed and shocked but the police thought he was the only person injured – until Dr Travers told his tale.

At half-past nine that night Aunt Rebecca Hoskins was sitting by her fire thinking aggrieved thoughts about the inconsiderateness of nieces who were asked to supper and never turned up when she was startled by a neighbour who burst in, exclaiming, "Have you heard about Sandy Pengelly, then, Mrs Hoskins? Terrible thing, poor little soul, and they don't know if she'm likely to live. Police have got the truck-driver that hit her – ah, it didn't ought to be allowed, speeding through the place like that at umpty miles an hour, they ought to jail him for life, not that that'd be any comfort to Bert and Jean."

Horrified, Aunt Rebecca put on a coat and went down to her brother's house. She found the family with white, shocked faces; Bert and Jean were about to drive off to the hospital where Sandy had been taken, and the twins were crying bitterly. Lob was nowhere to be seen. But Aunt Rebecca was not interested in dogs; she did not enquire about him.

"Thank the lord you've come, Beck," said her brother. "Will you stop the night with Don and the twins? Don's out looking for Lob and dear knows when we'll be back; we may get a bed with Jean's mother in Plymouth."

"Oh, if only I'd never invited that poor child," wailed Mrs Hoskins. But Bert and Jean hardly heard her.

That night seemed to last for ever. The twins cried them-selves to sleep. Don came home very late and grim-faced. Bert and Jean sat in a waiting room of the Western Counties Hospital, but Sandy was unconscious, they were told, and she remained so. All that could be done for her was done. She was given transfusions to replace all the blood she had lost. The broken bones were set, and put in slings and cradles.

"Is she a healthy girl? Has she a good constitution?" the emergency doctor asked.

"Aye, doctor, she is that," said Bert hoarsely. The lump in Jean's throat prevented her from answering; she merely nodded.

"Then she ought to have a chance. But I won't conceal from you that her condition is very serious, unless she shows signs of coming out from this coma."

But hour succeeded hour, and Sandy showed no sign of recovering consciousness. Her parents sat in the waiting room with haggard faces; sometimes one of them would go out to telephone the family at home, or to try and get a little sleep at the home of Grandma Pearce, not far away.

At noon next day Dr and Mrs Travers went to the Pengelly cottage to inquire how Sandy was doing, but the report was gloomy: "Still in a very serious condition." The twins were miserably unhappy. They forgot that they had sometimes called their elder sister bossy, and only remembered how often she had shared her pocket money with them, how she read to them and took them for picnics and helped with their homework. Now there was no Sandy, no Mother and Dad, Don went around with a grey, shuttered face, and, worse still, there was no Lob.

The Western Counties Hospital is a large one, with dozens of different departments and five or six connected buildings, each with three or four entrances. By that afternoon it became noticeable that a dog seemed to have taken up position outside the hospital, with the fixed intention of getting in. Patiently he would try first one entrance and then another, all the way round, and then begin again. Sometimes he would get a little way inside, following a visitor, but animals were, of course, forbidden, and he was always kindly but firmly turned

142

out again. Sometimes the porter at the main entrance gave him a pat or offered him a bit of sandwich – he looked so wet and beseeching and desperate. But he never ate the sandwich. No one seemed to own him or to know where he came from; Plymouth is a large city and he might have belonged to anybody.

At tea-time Grandma Pearce came through the pouring rain to bring a flask of hot tea with brandy in it to her daughter and son-in-law. Just as she reached the main entrance the porter was gently but forcibly shoving out a large, agitated, soaking-wet Alsatian dog.

"No, old fellow, you can *not* come in. Hospitals are for people, not for dogs."

"Why, bless me," exclaimed old Mrs Pearce. "That's Lob. Here, Lobby boy!"

Lob ran to her, whining. Mrs Pearce walked up to the desk.

"I'm sorry, ma'am, you can't bring that dog in here," the porter said.

Mrs Pearce was a very determined old lady. She looked the porter in the eye.

"Now, see here, young man. That dog has walked twenty miles from St Killan to get to my granddaughter. Dear knows how he knew she was here, but it's plain he knows. And he ought to have his rights! He ought to get to see her! Do you know," she went on, bristling, "that dog has walked the length of England – *twice* – to be with that girl? And you think you can keep him out with your fiddling rules and regulations?"

"I'll have to ask the Medical Officer," the porter said.

"You do that, young man." Grandma Pearce sat down in a determined manner, shutting her umbrella, and Lob sat patiently dripping at her feet. Every now and then he shook his head, as if to dislodge something heavy that was tied round his neck.

Presently a tired, thin, intelligent-looking man in a white coat came downstairs, with an impressive, silver-haired man in a dark suit, and there was a low-voiced discussion. Grandma

Pearce eyed them, biding her time.

"Frankly . . . not much to lose," said the older man. The man in the white coat approached Grandma Pearce.

"It's strictly against every rule, but as it's such a serious case we are making an exception," he said to her quietly. "But only *outside* her bedroom door – and only for a minute or two."

Without a word, Grandma Pearce rose and stumped up-stairs. Lob followed close to her skirts, as if he knew his hope lay with her.

They waited in the green-floored corridor outside Sandy's room. The door was half shut. Bert and Jean were inside. Everything was terribly quiet. A nurse came out. The white-coated man asked her something and she shook her head. She had left the door ajar and through it could be seen a high narrow bed with a lot of framework above it. Sandy lay there, very flat under the covers, very still. Her head was turned away. All Lob's attention was riveted on the bed. He strained towards it, but Grandma Pearce grasped his collar firmly.

"I've done a lot for you, my boy, now you behave yourself," she whispered grimly. Lob let out a faint whine, anxious and pleading.

At the sound of that whine Sandy stirred, just a little. She sighed, and moved her head the least fraction. Lob whined again. And then Sandy turned her head right over. Her eyes opened, looking at the door.

"Lob?" she murmured – no more than a breath of sound. "Lobby boy?"

The doctor by Grandma Pearce drew a quick sharp breath. Sandy moved her left arm – the one that was not broken – from below the covers, and let her hand dangle down, feeling, as she always did in the mornings, for Lob's furry head. The doctor nodded slowly.

"All right," he whispered. "Let him go to the bedside. But keep a hold on him."

Grandma Pearce and Lob moved to the bedside. Now she could see Bert and Jean, white-faced and shocked, on the far side of the bed. But she didn't look at them. She looked at the smile on her grand-daughter's face as the groping fingers found Lob's wet ears and gently pulled them. "Good boy," whispered Sandy, and fell asleep again.

Grandma Pearce led Lob out into the passage. There she let go of him and he ran off swiftly down the stairs. She would have followed, but Bert and Jean had come out into the passage, and she spoke to Bert fiercely.

"*I* don't know why you were so foolish as not to bring the dog before! Leaving him to find the way here all by himself – "

"But, Mother!" said Jean Pengelly. "That can't have been Lob. What a chance to take! Suppose Sandy hadn't – " She stopped, with her handkerchief pressed to her mouth.

"Not Lob? I've known that dog nine years! I suppose I ought to know my own grand-daughter's dog?"

"Listen, Mother," said Bert. "Lob was killed by the same truck that hit Sandy. Don found him – when he went to look for Sandy's school bag. He was – he was dead. Ribs all smashed. No question of that. Don told me on the phone – he and Will Hoskins rowed a half-mile out to sea and sank the dog with a lump of concrete tied to his collar. Poor old boy. Still – he was getting on. Couldn't have lasted for ever."

"*Sank him at sea?* Then what – ?"

Slowly old Mrs Pearce, and then the other two, turned to look at the trail of dripping wet footprints that led down the hospital stairs.

In the Pengellys' garden they have a stone, under the palm tree. It says: "Lob. Sandy's dog. Buried at sea."

KATYA, THE CROCODILE AND THE SCHOOL PETS

Sara Corrin

(*Adapted from Stephen Corrin's translation of the Russian original by K. Gernyet and G. Jagdfeld*)

About five years before the time this story begins, when Mitya had only just started school, his father, a ship's captain, had brought back a strange-looking egg from somewhere in Africa. Nobody, not even Father himself, knew what kind of egg it was, nor even whether it was alive or not. But, just in case, they stored it away in a basket, covered it with cotton wool and laid it beside the warm radiator.

It lay there for a very long while. Then, one day, Mitya discovered an empty shell in the basket, and in the dark corner under the radiator a small odd-looking creature, something between a lizard and a legendary dragon. It was a baby crocodile.

Mitya soon became the best-known boy in his school. Big boys from the upper school, as well as his own classmates, would come running to have a peep at his pet crocodile. There was a special article in the newspaper, entitled 'Our Guest from Africa' and a photograph of Mitya and his crocodile. His mother kept a copy of the newspaper in her handbag and showed the article to all her friends. She was particularly taken with the animal because it provoked such amazement in everybody. "Why not let the creature live? It's nice having one's own amphibian in the house," she would say.

147

Gradually they all got used to it and inquisitive visitors stopped coming in to see it. It lived in the house like any other domestic animal, crawled about wherever it pleased and swam – first in the washtub, and later in the bath.

But as the crocodile grew larger and larger Mother liked it less and less, and things became more and more unpleasant for Mitya. For some reason or other he was held to blame when the crocodile nibbled away half of Mother's nylon stocking or when the young woman who came to read the electric meter almost had an attack of hysterics when a monster about a yard long came creeping out of the dark passage. There were lots more incidents of this kind, not very pleasant to relate.

But the very worst disaster of all began when Mitya's father gave him an *Encyclopaedia of Animals*. Naturally the first thing he did was to read through everything it had to say on the subject of crocodiles. And then he rather rashly went and told his mother that their particular crocodile was very likely a giant Madagascar specimen, to be found south of the Limpopo. Limpopo left Mother unperturbed, but at the word "giant" she grew pale.

That same evening, as soon as Mitya had dropped off to sleep, Mother grabbed hold of the Encyclopaedia and began to read the article on TESTACEOUS LIZARDS. And she straight away came to the very thing she had been afraid of: ". . . Not infrequently people in flat-bottomed boats have been seized by crocodiles . . . they devour them quietly in the evening or at night and for this purpose they drag them away to a secluded spot on the river bank . . ." "How perfectly frightful," said Mother. "To think one could fall asleep peacefully in one's bed and wake up cornered like that in some isolated spot." When she came to the bit "Madagascar crocodile may attain a length of some ten yards," she closed the book with a bang. She had had enough.

All that night she didn't sleep a wink and first thing next morning she demanded that the crocodile be cleared out of the house. And although Mitya, Encyclopaedia in hand, pointed out that the learned writer himself considered the figure of ten yards to be somewhat exaggerated, Mother insisted that if it were not true the Encyclopaedia would never have allowed it to be put in. Even when Mitya read aloud to her that crocodiles attain such dimensions only when they reach the age of a hundred, Mother declared that this was a pre-Revolution edition and that the Encyclopaedia was now out of date.

From then on Mother would regularly creep up to the crocodile and measure it with a tape measure. This went on until once it nearly bit her finger. So then she took to guessing its length by looking at it. But that made matters worse, because it turned out that the crocodile seemed to have put on another half-yard every time she looked.

When spring came, things took a turn for the worse. At the end of term they began to do some repairs to the school buildings. The animals had to be distributed among various children and Mitya took home two rabbits, a tortoise and a starling which could say "Hullo" and "Quick March".

Because of the crocodile, however, the atmosphere at home was very strained and the animals were received without enthusiasm. Mitya gave his word of honour that in the autumn he would surrender the crocodile to the school together with the other animals. That was the first thing. Secondly, he had to guarantee that the crocodile would not damage or spoil

any single thing in the house. In return for this Mother agreed to put up with the animals until August 31st.

But the very next morning (when our story begins) this is what took place.

Mother and Mitya were drinking tea. Mother had taken the milk-jug and was pouring milk into her cup. Suddenly the cup started edging sideways and the stream of milk began pouring on to the table-cloth. At the same time the sugar-basin and the pot of jam also began to edge sideways at an ever-increasing speed. The cloth sidled away as though it were alive. With a loud clatter, dishes, cutlery and everything else on the table went showering on to the floor.

Mother grabbed the creeping end of the cloth and pulled it towards her. The tea poured from the overturned cups and jam oozed all over the place. Mother kept tugging. Above the table appeared the jaws of the crocodile, clinging to the cloth. Mitya grabbed hold of the crocodile and finally managed to pull it away – with a large portion of cloth in its mouth.

"It's a madhouse!" shrieked Mother.

"Hullo!" chirped the starling merrily from its cage.

This inoffensive little word was the last straw. Her patience at an end, Mother said in a voice of steel: "Out with the lot of 'em! Get your whole menagerie out of here!"

150

"How do you mean, my whole menagerie!" asked Mitya indignantly. "The rabbits have got nothing to do with this. Nor the tortoise. They've done no harm!"

"Out with the lot!" repeated Mother firmly. "Either they go or I go."

So there sat Mitya on his doorstep with all his animals, looking gloomily into space, wondering what to do next.

Down the sunlit avenue tripped Katya Patushkov, bouncing her ball. As though attached to an invisible elastic, it leapt backwards and forwards from the ground to Katya's nimble hand. She was terribly clever at making the ball always land on the sunny patches and never in the shade. "Three hundred and five . . . three hundred and six . . ." she counted silently. None of the girls who lived in the block of flats surrounding her yard, or in the whole of the street was better at it than Katya. So off she trotted down the next street where as yet nobody knew her, cleverly changing the direction of her bounces from left to right and from right to left. Then,

151

suddenly, quite out of the blue, a small boy came running up and gave the ball a hefty kick.

The ball soared upwards, flew down the street, landed among a flock of pigeons and then bounced against a wall and rolled along to rest at the foot of a lamp-post. "I'll give him what for!" cried Katya, dashing off after the lad. But he had run away to hide behind his grandmother and from there shook his fist at her. "Coward!" said Katya. "Coward! Coward! Coward!" and set off after her ball. She bent down to pick it up when "Gosh!" she exclaimed and raised her hands in astonishment. She was looking straight into the eyes of a snow-white rabbit. Its red eyes were fixed on Katya. Behind this rabbit sat another, its long ears spread out along its back.

The rabbit hutch stood on the first step of a short flight in front of a door. On the second step was another cage. In this one a bird was hopping about and twisting its head to gaze at Kayta.

On the top step sat a boy, Mitya of course, gazing gloomily and steadfastly straight in front of him. On his knees lay a violet-coloured shoe-box in the lid of which a slot had been cut out. A live animal of some kind was quietly scraping away inside. At the feet of this strange boy lay a long case on which, painted in bright red letters, was the word "CROQUET". Katya glanced at him cautiously. She would have been far wiser to have picked up her ball and gone on her way. But she couldn't resist the rabbits; they looked so pretty. And what on earth could be hidden in the shoe-box, or in the croquet case? And why should all these animals be out in the street?

Katya could not bring herself to leave. She lingered for a while, gazing at the lad, who never moved but kept staring glumly in front of him. She tiptoed up to the rabbits and gently felt one pinkish nose through the bars. "Don't touch!" said the boy hoarsely.

"Can't I just stroke it?" begged Katya.

"Leave them alone!" was the reply.

Through the slot of the shoe-box peeped a head, turning this way and that and then hiding. "Ooh!" exclaimed Katya.

"It's a little snake!"

"Snake yourself!" muttered the boy. And although the words were harsh, his voice seemed just a shade less angry. Apparently Katya's admiration did not wholly displease him. He even went so far as to open the box slightly and Katya was able to catch a glimpse of a tortoise. The creature poked out its snake-like head and scratched feebly with its paws against the cardboard walls, trying to get out of its cramped quarters.

"Oh!" exclaimed the girl, and reaching out towards the animal she stumbled over the box and fell sprawling all over it.

The boy seized her by the arm, dragged her away from the box, and shouted: "Where do you think you're going? Go back to where you came from!"

But Katya couldn't bear to go away. There was definitely something else in the croquet box, though it was impossible to make out anything through the very tiny slit (which had probably been cut to let the air in). She put on her most thoughtful expression, and said, as though to herself but just loud enough for the boy to hear: "Anyone can see he's just putting on airs. He hasn't really got anything very terrifying in that box."

The boy gave a contemptuous grunt and shrugged his shoulders. "Aha!" thought Katya. "It's beginning to work!" She took a deep breath and began again in her nastiest tone: "Fancy! He wants us to think he's got a shark in there . . . or a tiger . . . or . . . a crocodile . . ."

"Crocodile," repeated the lad gloomily. Katya laughed with all the scorn she could muster.

"Crocodile," said the lad once again.

"It's really disgusting, the fibs he tells!" said Katya.

"Fibs? Just have a look for yourself!" exclaimed the boy, drawing back the lid of the box. Inside lay a live crocodile, and then the whole story came pouring out.

When Katya heard the sad tale, she began to feel very sorry for Mitya, sorry for the homeless animals, even sorry for the

153

crocodile; after all, he couldn't help being a crocodile and not a kitten.

"What will you do now?" she asked.

"I don't know," said Mitya. "I'm trying to think."

Katya stood up and clasped her hands together. "I know what!" she said. "Give them to me. They'll be all right. Honestly they will. I'll look after them."

For quite a long while Mitya said not a word. Then he asked: "What about your parents?"

"Oh, they're fine. And besides they aren't at home."

"Are there any small girls around the house?" asked Mitya suspiciously.

"Yes, there are," admitted Katya. "There's my little sister Milka. But she's at nursery school till half past five. And I won't let her hurt them. I promise I won't."

Mitya was once again lost in thought. Finally, he said: "Well, it's like this. I can't let you have them for the whole of the summer, of course. I daren't. They're school property. You understand, don't you? You see, you don't go to our school." Katya sighed. "But until tonight," continued Mitya, "while I go to see one of my friends out in the country, I might be able to let you have them." Katya fairly beamed.

"Now look," said the boy sternly. "You've got to remember you are taking official property into your care."

"I shall remember," promised Katya, clasping her hands tightly together.

"And you know how closely you have to guard them?"

"Right," said Katya. "I shall guard this state property with my life."

"You must make an inventory of the animals and give me a receipt," warned the boy, and Katya agreed.

Mitya took the box containing the crocodile and the hutch with the two rabbits. Katya carried her ball in one hand, the starling in its cage in the other, and under her arm the box with the tortoise.

They didn't have far to go — just along a couple of streets. They went up to the third floor and there on one of the doors hung a small card with the words: J. P. PASTUSHKOV. "Well, here we are," said Katya and brought out a key which she carried on a string tied round her waist.

"Are you quite certain there's no one at home?" asked Mitya.

"Positive," Katya assured him. "Mother's out shopping. Granny's at the market and Father's at a rehearsal. And of course Milka's at the nursery school." She opened the door, and the very first thing they heard were the tender strains of a violin. Mitya looked at Katya with an expression of the utmost severity. "I don't know why Dad's at home," she muttered glumly. "They've probably cancelled his rehearsal or something."

Mitya grunted distrustfully and they both tiptoed down the passage. From a cupboard in the wall Grandmother's white cat stared at them with gleaming eyes. Then they went into Katya's room. Toy bricks lay scattered about on the floor and against the wall ticked an old pendulum-clock with a cat's face above the dial, the eyes moving non-stop from side to side. Under the clock stood a child's bed and in it a five-year-old girl was sleeping peacefully.

Katya, horrified, gazed at the sleeping Milka and Mitya looked bitterly at Katya. It was all perfectly clear: she had deceived him, lured him into her house in order to gain possession of the animals.

But Katya had not been deceiving him. How could she have known that that day a little boy had fallen ill at Milka's school and all the children had been sent home as a precaution?

She placed the starling and tortoise on the floor, and tried as hard as she could to prove her innocence. But Mitya was not even listening. He had made up his mind to leave without further ado. He seized the hutch, the box and the case. But the box slipped from his hands. And when he tried to pick the tortoise up again, the crocodile-box fell with a crash. He tried balancing it on his shoulder but found he couldn't manage a cage, a hutch and a box with only two hands. Katya was sobbing quietly. Mitya looked at her, at the hutch and the cage, and suddenly gave the whole thing up as hopeless. "Make out the receipt!" he ordered.

Beaming with joy, Katya rushed to the table. She tore out a page from her arithmetic exercise-book and got her pen ready. The boy dictated and she took down his words, trying hard to make as few mistakes as possible. Then she signed her name: Katya. But Mitya protested that you can't write "Katya" on a receipt; you've got to write "Katherine" because it's a document. So she signed properly and handed him the receipt.

This is how it read:

angora Rabbits 2.
European tortoise 1.
Madagascar Crocodile 1.
talking Starling 1.
I promise to return the above property safe and intact.
~~Katia~~
Katherine Pastushkov.

"And what words can the starling say?" asked Katya.

"Oh, just one or two things," replied the boy casually, as he carefully blotted the paper, folded it in four and stuffed it into his pocket. "Got any roots?" he asked.

"'Fraid not," said Katya, rather scared.

"Then you'll have to give the rabbits oats."

"Right."

"Have you got a bath?"

"Yes."

"Put the crocodile in it."

The music coming from Father's study suddenly came to a stop. Mitya looked a bit uneasy and said: "Well, I'll be off now. Look after them."

"Oh yes, I certainly shall," Katya assured him. She closed the door behind him; she was alone with the animals. She carried the box with the crocodile into the bathroom, turned on the tap and dropped the animal in. It flopped about in the water, splashing her all over. Then she poured some fresh water into a basin for the starling. "Hullo!" chirped the bird. Katya laughed joyfully. She pulled the tortoise out of its narrow box and transferred it to the crocodile's. "Now have a little stroll," she said to it.

Next she ran to the kitchen, where she shook all the bags and jars and peeped into every sack and box. There were definitely no oats in the house. She would have to run out to the shops. But what about money? Get some from Father? From his study musical sounds could once again be heard. He was playing a piece called "The Devil's Trill" and whenever he played that not even Grandmother dared disturb him and Milka used to be sent out for a walk. Katya reflected for a minute. "Oh, aren't I stupid!" she said suddenly and took down from the shelf the china piggy-bank in which they were saving up for a magic lantern. She shook it over the table until there was a whole pile of coppers and silver. Just then Milka began tossing in her bed. Katya was worried. How could she leave Milka alone with the animals? She dared not trust them with her. But Milka was once more sleeping sweetly and Katya decided she wouldn't wake up anyway. To run to the shops and back would take ten minutes at most.

"Could I please have some oats for rabbits?" Katya asked the shopkeeper.

"Sorry, I've only got some oatmeal," he replied.

"All right then, I'll take the oatmeal," Katya said. "It's for rabbits, you know, it's their ration. But my tortoise doesn't eat oats. Then there's my crocodile. You can't imagine what he's like. He even bites people's shoes in two."

All the customers were staring at her, and one young lad, carrying a whole chain of ring-shaped bread rolls slung around his shoulder and a bag of macaroni in his hand, stepped right up to her and glared at her as though she chewed up shoes herself. . . . And when Katya went out of the shop, the boy followed close on her heels, chewing a bread-ring as he walked and not taking his eyes off her. Katya hurried as fast as she could. She ran across the road, turned the corner and went running towards the *Neptune* cinema. People were crowding to get in. All of a sudden she spied Tanya just walking through the cinema entrance. Tanya was her very closest friend. "Wait for me, Tanya!" she cried. "I've got something to tell you!" But Tanya had already disappeared through the doors. Did this mean that Tanya was not going to know anything about Katya's animals? Well, that would be a fine friendship! To have a live crocodile in your own home and not even to show the tip of its tail to your best friend!

With these thoughts buzzing through her head, Katya dashed in straight after her friend. "Ticket," shouted the girl at the door and attempted to stop Katya, but she wriggled past and got lost in the crowd. "Tanya!" she cried, but there was so much noise that her voice was drowned. The boy with the bread-rings and the macaroni had followed Katya and leaned against a wall near the exit of the cinema. He unthreaded another ring from his chain and began munching leisurely, waiting for her.

The ticket-girl couldn't leave her post to give chase to Katya, who was picking her way through the crowd, craning her neck to see Tanya. She caught sight of her taking her seat in a row by the wall. "Tanya!" she called. "I haven't got much time. I've got some animals at home." And she rapidly proceeded to tell her friend the important details. Just then the lights dimmed.

"Sit down!" shushed everybody from behind and both girls sat down on to one seat, while Katya hurriedly began her story once more. By this time Tanya had got the hang of the situation. "A crocodile!" she whispered excitedly. "A talking one! Let's go!" And they began groping their way towards the exit. Now there were irate whisperings from all sides, but it was when they reached the doors that the real trouble started. The ticket-girl flatly refused to open the doors.

"You may leave when *The Golden Fish* is over and not a minute before."

The girls looked at the screen and saw that the old man was only just getting ready to cast his net into the sea for the first time. The usherette pointed to a couple of empty seats. "Sit down there!"

Then Katya lost her temper. She didn't like being shouted at even when it was done in a whisper. She shouted back at the usherette, also in a whisper. "It's only people with tickets who've got to stay till the end! I've no ticket. You've got no right to make me sit through to the end of *The Golden Fish*. You ought to show me out! Shame on you for not doing your duty!"

"What d'you mean, you've got no ticket! Show me your ticket!" said the usherette hoarsely, in a state of utter bewilderment.

"I haven't got one," whispered Katya with some pride, and the ticket-girl, without another word, opened the doors and let them through . . . They slipped into the foyer and rushed to the exit.

"Ah, here comes the girl without a ticket," gloated the young woman in the box-office. "Have they kicked you out?" Katya could have given a nasty reply to that if she'd wanted to. But she was in no mood to start explaining and out they rushed into the street.

The lad with the bread-rings detached himself from his leaning-post and followed them.

Katya was anxious to feed the rabbits, and they were quite near her house when Tanya suddenly started to run over to the other side of the street. "Where are you off to?" asked Katya.

"That's where she lives."

"Who?"

"Lilia, of course."

"Are we really going to Lilia's?"

Tanya stopped in the middle of the road. "Well, of course,

what do you think? Don't you remember, when the film-star came to her sister's house, she fetched us right away? We can't hide the crocodile from her."

Katya felt ashamed. She said: "Very well, then. Only let's be as quick as we can, because it's already time to give the rabbits their food."

The girls looked up to Lilia's window and called out in unison: "Li-lia!" But she did not appear. Again they shouted and again nothing happened. When they had collected enough breath to call again they heard a deafening roar just behind them: LI-LIA! It was the boy with the macaroni yelling at the top of his voice. He was standing just a little way away. Immediately Lilia's head poked out from behind a pot of flowers.

"Lilia, quick! Come and see what I've got," cried Katya. "Come quickly! I've got some animals!"

"Can't hear you," shouted Lilia in reply.

Katya and Tanya looked at each other in despair and then at the boy with the macaroni, who immediately grasped the situation. Transferring his bag of macaroni to his other hand, he puffed out his chest, put his hand to his mouth and yelled: "Come down right away. Come and see my crocodile."

"I'll be right down," answered Lilia and her head disappeared.

Katya was desperate to get back home. She had to feed the rabbits. But Lilia declared she would not go a single step farther without Shura. The rabbits wouldn't die (she said) and Shura might be mortally offended. . . . Friends didn't behave like that, she said. "And may I perish on this very spot," she affirmed, "if Shura is not this very moment sitting somewhere on a bench in the avenue reading *The Headless Rider*." The girls tore along the avenue, the boy with the macaroni silently following behind, munching yet another bread-ring as he went.

Shura was, in fact, sitting on a park-bench reading *The Headless Rider*. "What did I tell you?" said Lilia triumphantly.

"Listen, Shura. You'll die when you've heard what I've got to tell you!"

Shura did not die, but a nursemaid sitting next to her and carrying an infant-in-arms very nearly did. While the girls vied with one another to tell Shura about the crocodile and the starling, she kept gasping with excitement, and in her agitation she kept bouncing her baby higher and higher, so that if the story had gone on a little longer the poor creature would have found itself up in a tree.

"Are you certain it's not all a pack of lies?" she asked. "Come on then, let's go." And picking up the baby, she leaped up from the bench. And off they all ran.

In the street, blocking the path, was a big fat man with three enormous boxes on his head. In the opposite direction, clearing a path through the passers-by, came Katya with her little bag of oatmeal, followed by Tanya, Lilia, Shura, the nursemaid and baby, two other girls and the boy with the macaroni, now on his seventh bread-ring.

Then all of a sudden . . . Katya bumped right into the fat man with the boxes. "Ow!" roared the fat man. He toppled over and sat down on the pavement. The boxes capsized into the middle of Katya's group. The girls screamed and waved their arms. The boxes scattered all over the place and multi-coloured balls burst out of them and went bouncing about — balls of all sizes.

"Oh, I'm frightfully sorry!" said Katya, horrified, looking at the balls as they went rolling all over the avenue.

"Hooligans!" the fat man roared. "You walk along minding your own business and they come charging into you!"

The balls continued to roll in all directions while the girls helped the man to his feet and dusted him. But he pushed them aside and went on shouting: "One hundred and twenty-five! That's what's on the invoice! And now look what's happened!" He gazed down the avenue. All over the place, they were. Children were picking them up, starting a game, throwing them to one another. Some started football practice. School teams bobbed up from all corners.

The fat man suddenly stopped shouting and leaning his head to one side took a long look at the jolly scene. "Come on, kids!" he roared, beginning to enjoy it all, and made a dash to collect the balls. Katya and all her companions rushed to help him. Children and their mothers and grandmothers were all gathering up the balls and fetching them to him. And the fat man was counting: "Ninety-four, thank you. Ninety-five, thank you. Ninety-six, much obliged." At this point, Tanya decided to take charge. She received the balls and passed them over to Katya, Shura, Lilia, the two other girls and the macaroni boy. The fat man was beaming all over as he counted: "One hundred and twenty-four, one hundred and twenty-five. That's the lot! . . . A hundred and twenty-six," he added, and suddenly stopped, quite flabbergasted.

"How many did you say there were?" asked Katya.

"A hundred and twenty-five. That's what's on the invoice."

They were all astonished and started counting the balls all over again. There were indeed a hundred and twenty-six. Where on earth had the extra one come from? That was to remain a mystery . . . The fat man replaced the lids on the

boxes and planted them on his head, and made his way to the shop called "The Children's World".

And so the whole procession moved off, Katya hugging her bag of oatmeal; she sighed bitterly as she thought of the slumbering Milka and the hungry rabbits.

While Katya was out buying the oats, Milka slept peacefully. The crocodile was swimming in the bath, the starling was hopping about and chirping "Hullo" and "Quick March" to the flies around his cage, and the tortoise was crawling round in the croquet-box, which, after the shoe-box, it found most roomy. The rabbits were nibbling the last few dandelions left in the hutch.

Father, as usual, had got lost at the thirty-seventh bar of "The Devil's Trill" and was starting all over again. In short, everything was quiet and peaceful.

But just at that very moment, a ray of sunshine fell on Milka's face. She rubbed her eyes with her fists, sneezed and awoke. For a long while she lay screwing up her eyes and stretching, until she finally opened her eyes properly. And then she saw the bird, the rabbits and the tortoise. Milka jumped out of bed and ran towards them. She was five years old and wasn't particularly puzzled about where they had come from, or why they happened to be in her room. She was simply happy that they were there. She squatted down by the rabbits and poked a finger inside the hutch.

"Quick march!" chirped the starling. Milka looked at it and nodded; she had understood immediately. The little bird was playing "school". It was taking the teacher's part and giving orders in the morning exercises. "Jolly good!" agreed Milka. She stood at attention for the exercise and marched round the room, trying to keep time to the beat of "The Devil's Trill", the music of which wafted in from Father's study. All entangled in her long nightie, Milka kept marching on. She was waiting for teacher to give the command "Stop!" and start another exercise. But the starling wasn't even thinking about saying "Stop!" It suddenly jumped into the little basin of water,

fluttering its wings and splashing water all over the place. Milka saw what "teacher" was doing and got very angry.

"We haven't finished the march yet and you're washing already!" she cried. "You mustn't wash yet. I had better be teacher and you . . ." And so that the starling should agree to let her have the teacher's part, Milka was already thinking out something interesting for it to do. "You can be on duty at the wash-basin."

"Hullo!" cried the bird.

"Good-morning, children," said Milka very importantly, addressing the rabbits and the tortoise. She started to clap her hands. "Children, we are now going for a walk," she commanded in her best teacher's voice. She opened the hutch and helped the rabbits hop out.

They began jumping about the room. One of them hid under the bed and the other under Katya's table. "Don't scamper about, children," cried Milka, but they paid no attention. She then opened the door for the starling but it refused to fly out. "Just look how this boy is dawdling," she said indignantly. She pulled the bird out of the cage, but it struggled from her hand and flew up to the ceiling. The tortoise proved to be the most obedient pupil. When Milka pulled it out of its box and placed it on the floor it drew its head under its shell and sat there very quietly. "That's a good girl," said Milka approvingly.

She placed the tortoise in her largest doll's bed, covered it up with a blanket and tucked it cosily in. It made no attempt to run off anywhere and Milka liked it more and more. "You

164

shall be my daughter," she told it. "Sleep, my little one, sleep", and she hummed it a little tune. And while she sang and rocked her "daughter" to sleep, first one rabbit and then the other slipped through the open door into the passage. Milka didn't even notice.

Milka was wheeling her doll's pram about in the courtyard. Inside lay the tortoise wrapped in a blanket. "Don't sit up or you'll catch cold," said Milka sternly, giving the pram a little shake. Suddenly the tortoise began to move over and spread itself over the pillow. "Now don't be naughty," she said and tried to push it back, but it bit her finger. "O you. . . .!" she cried angrily.

Lev, a little boy from the next street, came running up. "Say!" he exclaimed, looking at the animal. "Now that's really something!"

"It's nasty!" said Milka through her tears.

"I'll swap you my magnet for it," offered Lev.

"No!"

"How about this half of a pair of scissors? It can still cut."

"No!" said Milka again.

"Well, what else do you want?" Lev turned out his pockets and emptied all his treasures straight on to the ground. Both children squatted down and began to rummage among them. The boy picked out each one separately and praised it shame-lessly and dishonestly. "Terrific lens, this. It's a magnifying glass. You can set fire to anything you like with it. Shall I burn a hole in your dress?"

"No!" Milka shook her head vigorously. "What else have you got there, in that little box? I'll have the ribbons!" She seized the little box and Lev was amazed to get the tortoise so cheaply. He not only gave her the ribbons but generously added a piece of sealing-wax. And Milka began to lay out her coloured ribbons triumphantly on the bench.

Katya's grandmother had finished all her shopping and was coming back from the market. She was climbing up to her flat on the third floor when she met her neighbour coming out of her flat carrying a bowl full of wet washing. "Good morning, Miss Slovenka," said Grandmother warmly.

"Your cat has been sniffing at my milk," said Miss Slovenka, pursing her lips. "How many times have I asked you not to let it run along the ledge outside my balcony. Anybody that can't look after a cat shouldn't keep one."

"I'm terribly sorry!" muttered Grandmother.

The door of her neighbour's flat remained slightly ajar. Grandmother put down her heavy basket and started to look for her key. She accidentally knocked the basket over, and the onions bobbed out and went capering down the steps. "Silly Billy that I am," said Grandmother and went back down to gather them up. The door of the Patushkovs' flat burst open and through it flew a white rabbit which described an arc and flopped straight into Grandmother's basket. Then the door slammed to.

The rabbit didn't seem to be distressed by its change of fortune. Burrowing in the basket, it picked out a nice carrot and began to nibble. And Grandmother, having collected her onions, climbed back up the stairs and suddenly spied the animal in her basket. "Oh, hullo there!" she said, wondering where on earth it could have come from. She squatted down by her basket, watched the rabbit munch the carrot with great gusto, and was touched. "My little pet, my little beauty," she cooed. Then she caught sight of Miss Slovenka's open door and everything became clear.

"Well she's a fine one," she said, shaking her head. "Telling others what do do!" Then, addressing the rabbit she said: "Well, you've had your meal and you've had your little stroll. Come along home, my dear, or you'll get lost." She ever so gently pushed the rabbit into her neighbour's flat and threw in a cabbage and a turnip after it. Then she carefully closed the door so that it would not run back out again. And now Grandmother had nothing left to put in her soup, but she was not in the least bit upset. "Never mind. I'll go and do some more shopping," she decided, and taking her basket she went downstairs.

166

When Miss Slovenka had hung out her washing on the line in the attic, she came back to her flat with her empty wash tub. She slammed the door behind her, stumbled over something round and hard, and fell with a crash to the floor. The tub flew from her hand and went rolling down the passage. She got up, switched on the light and saw a turnip and cabbage-head on the floor. She simply couldn't understand where these vegetables had come from, but she had no time to think about things like that now. "Hooligans!" she said angrily, and went into her room. She was getting ready to go on her holidays and was seeing to the last few things before her departure. An old tablecloth lay spread out in the centre of the room on the floor and on it lay two fur coats, a red fox fur, a white muff and a deerskin cap. She put on her hat, tied up her things in a bundle and set off to the storage depot to deposit them for safekeeping while she was on holiday.

She walked straight up to the man in charge of the storage depot, who inspected her things and said: "One male polecat fur coat," and noted it down on a receipt-slip. Then he drew out the second fur coat. Something dropped out of it. "We don't accept rabbits, madam," he said.

"What do you mean, rabbit?" said Miss Slovenka indignantly. "That's Australian kangaroo."

"Do you call this a kangaroo?" asked the man, lifting up a white rabbit by its ears.

For a moment Miss Slovenka was speechless and looked blankly at it. "Look here," she said finally, "whose leg are you pulling?"

"Madam," said the man sternly, tapping his pencil on the counter, "I am not going to argue. Please take your animal away."

Miss Slovenka flared up. "I have quite enough to put up with cats at home without having hares thrust at me here!" she cried. "Yours is the only depot where I've been offered a hare. Goodness knows why!"

"Madam," said the man. "In the first place, it is not a hare. It's a rabbit. In the second place, in so far as it fell out of your

167

coat, it is your rabbit. Had it fallen from mine," he added gently, as he looked at it, "it would have been mine."

But Miss Slovenka would have none of this. "I could understand if it were a moth. But rabbits in a fur coat!" She suddenly recalled that her door had been left open for a few moments while she had been up in the attic. "It would seem," she said rather faintly, "that my neighbours are capable of anything. I even know which one of them has done it. It's Mrs Medvedkin!" She grabbed the rabbit and wrapped it up in a cloth. And leaving the storage depot, she darted straight off home.

"It's all clear to me now," she mumbled to herself. "Mrs Medvedkin! That's who it is! All the neighbours are plotting against me. They all know that I simply can't stand animals and they've been deliberately pestering me with cats, dogs and rabbits. I'll get even with Mrs Medvedkin! I'll show her!" She rushed into the courtyard. She was tormented by the thoughts that the Medvedkins were at that very moment having a good laugh at her expense. She stole quietly up to the window of their flat and started to eavesdrop.

The Medvedkins were indeed having a chat, but what they were saying had nothing whatsoever to do with her. ". . . I think, perhaps, a cake. . . " Mrs Medvedkin was saying.

"Yes, of course, a cake . . . with cream. . . " said her son, Sasha, who was a pupil at the College of Music.

Mr Medvedkin then promised to send the cake with some-one from the office, because he himself would not be able to get back home in time. The talk on this topic came to an end, but for some reason or other Miss Slovenka was more than ever convinced that it was Mrs Medvedkin who had planted the rabbit in her flat. A plan for revenge began to brew in her mind and she rushed into her flat as fast as her legs could carry her.

As soon as she got inside she took out of the cupboard a cake-box, a length of tape and some ribbon. She placed the rabbit inside the box, surrounded it with cotton wool so that it shouldn't move about too much, made a little hole in one of the sides for ventilation and carefully tied up the box with the tape and ribbon. "With cream!" she sniggered to herself. Miss Slovenka then waited a little while – long enough, according to her reckoning, for Mr Medvedkin to go out and buy the cake and send it home from his office. Then she muffled herself up in an old shawl, went downstairs and rang the Medvedkins' bell. "From Mr Medvedkin," she said in a disguised voice and, hiding her face, thrust the cake-box through the door as it opened and then ran quickly off.

At Katya's home Father was standing in front of a one-legged music-stand on which lay a sheet of music. He was coming to the trickiest passage. As usual, at this point, his spectacles began to slide down his nose (they hung on very precariously by one side-piece). Spectacles and eternally creaking doors were two things that irritated Father immensely and prevented him from enjoying life. Having adjusted his spectacles, Father passed on to the tricky section. This was the tenderest part of the piece, played on the highest part of the strings. To achieve this Father would stretch his fingers right up to the bridge and play very gentle sounds, a bit like the peep of a bird.

Grandmother's white cat, dozing in the cupboard in the passage, would prick up its ears whenever it heard this section and get terribly excited because it imagined it to be the squeaking of a mouse. Although there were no mice in the house and it had never seen one in its life, it had always dreamed of catching one. And on this occasion, hearing the squeak, it leaped from the cupboard and began slinking stealthily towards Father's door, twitching its tail excitedly. Father heard the wretched door creak. He winced. Puss, whiskers all a-tremble, like a beast of prey on the prowl, thrust into the room. "Shoo!" shouted Father, brandishing his bow. Puss unhurriedly went out. Father resumed playing.

Hearing the squeak again, Puss turned back. Once more the door creaked. Father turned round furiously. His spectacles jumped from his nose to the ground and his eyes fell, not upon a cat, but on a blurred white patch. "Ah, so there you are!" said Father, seizing the cat by the scruff of its neck and flinging it into the passage. The offended cat crawled into the cupboard to keep company with the headless doll and a couple of building bricks. And there it remained, waving its tail with indignation. Father looked for his spectacles, cursing his confounded house full of insolent cats and creaking doors where a man couldn't have a moment's peace. He accidentally kicked his spectacles into a corner, gave it up as a bad job, and began to play without spectacles, bringing his nose right up against the page of music.

In the passage a white rabbit scuttled rapidly past the cat. At the sight of it, Puss began to spit, but to be on the safe side it buried itself a little deeper inside the cupboard. The rabbit pricked up its ears, pursed its lips, and hopped into Father's study.

For over five minutes now Father had been left undisturbed and he was beginning to feel a little calmer when suddenly there was that intolerable creak again. Beside himself with rage, he spun round and, of course, once more he saw a blurred white patch. "Get out!" he roared, making a grab at it. The rabbit hopped under the divan, but Father thought it was gone.

He took up his violin and, half-closing his eyes, he played the first note. He didn't get to the second. The door gave a horrible creak. Father went cold. Once again the white cat was in the room. "Not possible," he muttered, his bow falling from his hands. The "cat" moved insolently across the room in funny little hops, and hid under the divan. "That animal will drive me out of my mind, you'll see!" said Father gloomily and went out to look for a mop.

The second rabbit (for this was indeed it), sat peacefully under the divan and nibbled at some sea-grass which had fallen out of the mattress. But it didn't have time for much; in came Father armed with a mop.

"I'll get rid of that cat yet!" he said, poking the mop under the divan. The rabbit jumped out. Father seized it, thrust it into a cupboard in the room, quickly closed both doors and locked them.

170

By this time Father's nerves were at breaking point, and he decided to take some valerian to calm himself down. He made his way to the medicine chest and began fumbling among all the little phials and putting them to his nose. He kept picking up the wrong one – castor oil, cod-liver oil, surgical spirit . . . and becoming more and more edgy. Finally he did come across the correct phial. He reached down a glass, sat himself in an armchair and carefully began to pour out the drops, counting them in a whisper – "one, two, three . . ."

The real cat was sleeping in the cupboard in the passage. Now and again, in its sleep, it would give a sudden start and show its claws. It was probably dreaming that at long last, it had caught a mouse . . . Suddenly, it opened one eye and dilated its nostrils. It could scent a fascinating and irresistible odour. It was the valerian. Any cat is ready to run to the ends of the earth for valerian. Puss licked its lips, leaped from the cupboard and darted towards Father's room. Father was sitting in his armchair counting: ". . . ten . . . eleven . . . twelve . . . And at the very second that Father was saying "thirteen," Puss bounded into the room with its ghastly miaow.

Glass and phial fell from Father's hands. With a low rumbling purr the cat threw itself upon the drops of spilt valerian. "It's here again . . ." muttered Father faintly. He cast his eyes towards the cupboard in the room. The key was still in the lock!

He got up and tugged at the cupboard doors. They were both locked. He looked back at the cat once again and began to feel giddy. He simply failed to understand how one and the same cat could at one and the same time be both in the *locked* cupboard and loose in the room. Puss had by now licked the floor clean and was mewing plaintively, but there was no more valerian. It started to pace the room in a kind of drunken daze, and suddenly caught sight of itself in a large mirror. With a great hiss it rushed at its adversary, leaping up more than a yard in the air. Banging its head against the glass, it fell back to the floor, then scornfully turning its back on the mirror made for the opposite corner. On the way, for some reason or other, it jumped up on to the piano and from this height it observed on the wall a picture representing the continent of Africa. Puss decided to invade Africa. It sprang up and remained poised, clinging with one paw to a camel and with the other to a cloud. And all this – cat, picture, nail and string – fell to the ground with a crash.

Father sat in his armchair and gazed speechless at the cat. The cat, having done with Africa, emitted a savage war-cry and began to celebrate his victory. He found a ball and skidded along upon it, sped from cupboard to window, from window to stove and, in the course of all this, knocked over everything it was possible to knock over. "Never seen anything like it," said Father. "I know that things like this do *not* happen."

At that very second the starling flew into the room – the one Milka had let loose from its cage. Seeing the cat, it immediately flew to the ceiling. Father hadn't noticed it, but at this point he distinctly heard someone say, "Hullo". He pressed his fingers to his temples. "In the first place," he said, "I don't believe in fairy-tales. Secondly, there are no such things as miracles. There is a strictly scientific explanation for everything."

Puss sprang up on to the music stand and came toppling down with the music. "It's all perfectly simple," said Father. "What is happening here is something very ordinary indeed. . . ."

"Hullo!" called the starling from its ledge.

"A talking cat, that's what it is. A common hallucination. In normal cases, a cold compress should be applied to the head and the attack passes off." Father walked slowly to the door.

"Quick march," cried the starling.

"No hooliganism, please!" said Father sharply.

In the bathroom he took a Turkish towel from its hook, turned on the tap and bent over. From the water, a crocodile gazed straight into his eyes.

He collapsed on to a stool and sat for a while with eyes closed. Then he got up and tiptoed out of the room. He

172

walked up and down the passage, then stood for a while outside the bathroom. Then he opened the door with a jerk and peeped inside. The crocodile had not disappeared. It was wagging its tail and its toothy jaws were wide open. Father flung his towel over his shoulder and slowly returned to his room. He had decided that perhaps it would be best if he left the flat and got some fresh air. The first thing that met his eye was a white rabbit snugly asleep in his felt hat. But nothing really surprised him now. Giving up the whole thing as utterly hopeless, he turned his back on it and left the house, the towel still over his shoulder.

And the starling, whirling round the room, flew out through a small skylight.

Father had gone and the bath-tap was left running. Who could be bothered with taps when such things were going on in the house? And so the water in the bath kept rising and so did the crocodile with it, floating somewhat unsteadily on the surface. When he got high enough to reach the little soap shelf he swallowed the cake of IDEAL soap at one gulp and was about to turn his attention to a toothbrush when suddenly a small bird came and perched on the sill of the open window. The crocodile fixed it with its gaze and swam up closer. The bird blithely hopped along the sill. The water was now so high that the crocodile was able to crawl from the edge of the bath on to the window-sill. The bird watched it curiously, tilting its head to one side. The crocodile continued to crawl along the sill.

"Quick march!" cried the bird, whisked its tail and flew up into the blue sky. And the crocodile crawled on to the outer ledge above the street.

Miss Slovenka was standing by her window-sill washing her window. She was feeling cheerful. She was rubbing the window pane with a piece of cloth and singing. At that very moment the crocodile crawled past her window. She let out a faint shriek, collapsed and toppled over her bucket. The cloth hurtled from her hand down into the street below.

And, of course, it was bound to happen that just at that moment, Katya's father, Mr Pastushkov, should be slowly strolling along the street, still dazed by all the queer things that had happened to him. All of a sudden something wet brushed lightly against his cheek. Mechanically raising his hand, he found himself clutching a wet cloth. He looked at it gloomily, then continued his stroll, cloth in hand. At the corner he halted, and thrust his other hand into his pocket to get out his cigarettes. And suddenly he felt his case of spare spectacles! He had found them at last! The sun began to shine! The trees looked greener. How blue the sky had become, and how cheerfully the birds were twittering and the children playing and shouting! "What a lot of nonsense!" he said happily. "It was my eyes all the time!" At that instant, in the drainpipe close to where he was standing there was a loud crash. Father gave a start. The noise in the pipe got louder and louder. And from it emerged the jaws of a crocodile. Its body was stuck fast in the drainpipe.

Katya rushed home. She *must* feed the rabbits. She ran as fast as her legs could carry her. The others did not lag behind – Lilia, Tanya, Shura, two unknown girls, two strange boys, the nursemaid and the baby, and finally the boy with the macaroni, now finishing his eighth bread-ring. This time they managed to reach home without further incident. They arrived in the courtyard, and suddenly from somewhere up a tree somebody cried, "Hullo!" The starling was perched on the branch of a maple tree. Katya stood stock still. At first she couldn't grasp what had happened. Then she gave a low groan. "Public property," she whispered, in despair. The starling whisked its tail and disappeared into the sky. Katya burst into tears.

Milka was squatting by a bench, her empty doll's pram standing close by. She was placing the coloured ribbons on the bench and fitting them between the spaces. Each ribbon was a visitor and several had already arrived, "How are you?

Have some cake," she said, placing the screw and the sealing wax on a plate and offering it to them. At that instant Katya dashed past, sobbing. Behind her rushed the girls, and then the nursemaid brandishing the baby. Milka took fright. She pulled out her ribbons and, dragging her pram after her, rushed to follow the others. They dashed past Father, sitting on an old radiator near the front door, and he, hearing all the noise, merely looked up and watched glumly as his two daughters and all those unknown people tore past him screaming and yelling. "What a nightmare!" he sighed.

And not until the whole lot had got through the door did Father become really agitated. He sprang up and followed the girls, shouting: "Don't go inside!" But the whole throng ran straight upstairs. On the second floor they nearly swept Grandmother off her feet as she was coming back with her vegetables. Flashing past her, her eyes fairly bulging with fear, came Katya. And behind her, Milka, dragging her pram. And close on their heels Father with his towel and the whole crowd of complete strangers, tearing up as fast as they could. Grandmother did not lose her presence of mind. "Dial nine-nine-nine and ask for the Fire Brigade," she shouted, and joined in the chase.

Katya was the first to burst into the flat. On the floor lay the shoe-box and the croquet case. Both hutch and cage were empty. In the bath there was nothing but water, which flowed from the tap and ran out in a stream into the passage. Grandmother turned off the tap.

"The crocodile's gone," wailed Katya.

"She's been telling a lot of lies!" shouted the nursemaid indignantly. She gave the baby a spank and slammed the door.

Dissolved in tears, Katya looked at the empty cages. She knew Mitya was coming for the animals that evening; he had trusted her. Milka and Grandmother sat in silence, but Father was not downcast. As soon as he became aware of the *real* existence of the rabbits, the crocodile and the starling, all his

175

worries vanished as though by magic. Everything was now perfectly clear. "Enough tears," he said. "We are all going to take part in the search. And to start with we must first think where those rabbits could have got to."

Grandmother sighed and wrung her hands. "It's me, silly booby that I am. I know where it is. It was all my doing. . . . I must dash right away!" And out she ran on to the landing and disappeared.

"Excellent!" said Father. "So much for one rabbit. We must now figure out what could have become of the tortoise."

It was Milka's turn to break into tears. "I didn't know," she cried. "It bit me. . . . And I exchanged it . . ."

"Exchanged it?" asked Father.

"Yes," she admitted, and she drew out of her pram the coloured ribbons, the screw and the sealing wax.

"Well, go on then," cried the other girls, "go on then, go and change them back." The child briskly gathered up her treasures and, clasping them tightly, she made off as fast as her little legs could carry her.

"So much for the tortoise," said Father. "As for the crocodile, I'm going to take care of that one myself!" He found himself a broom and went out singing: "Crocodile, crocodile, little crocodile, here I come . . ."

The girls surrounded Katya. They had already been thinking out ways and means of recapturing the starling. Lilia had found Katya's butterfly-net. Tanya had made a lasso and Shura told Katya to get the net they used for a goal in netball. Then they all set off on the hunt.

Grandmother went straight to Miss Slovenka's and rang the bell. Miss Slovenka opened the door. "Sorry to trouble you," said Grandmother, somewhat embarrassed. "It's like this, you see . . ."

"You've arrived at just the right moment," said Miss Slovenka. "You can be a witness." She pulled Grandmother inside. "The Medvedkins are plotting to get rid of me. Look!" And she showed the cabbage-head and the turnip to Grandmother. "D'you see? They've purposely gone and left these things lying around to make me fall and get concussion!"

"That wasn't the Medvedkins," said Grandmother guiltily. "It was me."

"You!" she exclaimed. "And the rabbit? Was that you too?"

"And the rabbit," confessed Grandmother.

Miss Slovenka was almost choking with indignation. "And who does the crocodile belong to?"

"It's Katya's."

"Out of my house!" screamed Miss Slovenka, pushing Grandmother out and hurling the cabbage-head after her. "And that's the treatment I've given to your rabbit. And that's the treatment I'll give to anything that people stick in my house!" And she slammed the door in a fury.

Grandmother blinked and mechanically picked up the cabbage. She thought of Katya sobbing her eyes out, and she herself was on the verge of tears. But then she began to feel angry and started to bang at Miss Slovenka's door. "Impudent woman! Evil-minded creature!" shouted gentle Grandmother, banging the cabbage-head on the door. "Give me that rabbit back, d'you hear! You'll come to no good, I tell you! I won't allow you to upset the poor child." There was no reply. Somewhat ashamed of her unruly behaviour, Grandmother started to weep and went back home. "She's probably stewed it, and eaten it for dinner, the unscrupulous woman!" said Grandmother, sobbing bitterly.

Milka ran along the avenue with her treasures, looking for Lev. She couldn't find him anywhere, but she did know that he lived in a house with three courtyards, and that is where she went.

"Take these back and give us back our tortoise!" she cried.

Lev went on playing some indescribable tune. He paused to say: "Your tortoise? I've changed it for this mouth-organ."

"You had no right to; it belongs to school."

"Crikey!" said Lev. "Why didn't you come before?"

"I've been at home," said Milka, and went on to tell him

that Katya had other school animals, and that all of them had somehow or other disappeared.

"You're in a bad spot," said Lev. "Do you know what you can get for losing school property?"

"No," said Milka.

"They send you to prison," he said. Milka blinked. "It looks as though you're going to need a bit of help. You can thank your lucky stars you've got me. Let's go and find Gene."

And off they went into the next yard. Gene was sitting on the balcony with a book on his knees, laughing helplessly.

Lev called to him: "Go and fetch that tortoise."

"I swapped it with Valya for a copy of Baron Munchaüsen's *Tales.*"

Milka began crying and Lev explained very seriously why they *had* to have the tortoise back. He threw back the mouth-organ.

Gene rushed off at such a mad speed that he was soon out of sight. Lev grabbed Milka by the arm and pulled her along after him. They found Valya by the bank of the river. He was standing up to his knees in the water, holding a length of rope which was attached to the tortoise. The animal was swimming somewhere in the middle of the river. "That's our tortoise!" cried Milka. "You mustn't drown it! Fetch it out right away!"

"And where did you spring from?" enquired Valya. "The tortoise belongs to me."

"We swapped but we had no right to," explained Gene. "It belongs to school. Here, take back your Munchaüsen."

"Hm," said Valya spitefully. "What school?"

"No special one," said Milka. "It's school property."

"In that case, it's mine," said Valya, "and that's all there is to it."

Valya turned his back on them and began tugging at the rope, making the tortoise dive. "Pull in that rope. Do you hear?" said Lev. "We've already told you. The tortoise is school property!"

"It was!" said Valya, and started to whistle.

Lev struck Valya on the head and a struggle began. Valya

was tall and wiry, and things would have gone badly for Lev if Milka hadn't come running up just then and pulled Valya's hair. He gave a bellow and allowed the rope to slip from his hands. It disappeared beneath the water, and so did the tortoise. Milka started to scream and the boys were struck dumb.

"Here, hold this!" suddenly came the voice of the macaroni boy, who had followed the children when he saw them hunting for the tortoise. He thrust his bag into Milka's hand. He made a dash, plunged into the water and retrieved the helpless tortoise.

There was a large crowd at the corner. Everybody goggled at the crocodile's jaws protruding from the drainpipe. What on earth (everyone wondered) was a Madagascar crocodile doing in a domestic drainpipe? How did it get in and how was it going to be got out? One citizen declared that it must have escaped from the Zoo and was hiding from its pursuers. Another maintained that it had fallen from an aeroplane. Others reckoned that they were going to shoot a film, and that they'd put the crocodile there a little earlier so's he could get used to it. But the caretaker thought it was all a lot of nonsense. It wasn't a crocodile at all but simply someone playing the fool. Little boys in the crowd kept offering the animal bits of stick and wire and screamed with delight when it snapped its jaws. The only one to remain unastonished was the boy with the macaroni, who was now on the scene. He

179

stood very close to the pipe and stared enraptured at the crocodile which, at long last, had become reality. With some difficulty Father cleared a way through the crowd and finally found himself close enough to the drainpipe.

"Now we'll get it out," he said in a business-like tone, and waved the broom in front of the crocodile's muzzle. The animal snapped its jaws. "Come on, out you come!" The animal did not budge.

"How about pulling down the drainpipe? That should do the trick," suggested the boy with the macaroni.

Father suddenly glanced at him, then transferred his gaze to the string on which dangled his ring-shaped bread-rolls. "Hand me a roll or two," he said thoughtfully. The lad complied. Father threaded them on to the broomstick. Then, holding the stick at both ends, he raised it to the crocodile's jaws.

The monster opened its mouth and closed it with a bang, sinking its teeth into the rolls and the stick. Everybody then realized what Father was up to. Hands stretched out from all sides to grasp the ends of the broom. "Heave ho!" ordered Father, and everyone pulled. With quite unexpected gentleness, the animal slid down and out of the pipe and hung on to the stick without unclenching its teeth.

All the children cried "Hurrah!", and Father, the macaroni boy and a few volunteers triumphantly walked away with the stick and the clinging crocodile. Behind them followed the rest of the crowd. People's heads popped out from every window to gaze at this unusual spectacle. It was like being in a box at the theatre, but this was more interesting because they don't show you crocodiles in the theatre!

The girls were walking along the avenue scattering crumbs and crying "Tweet! Tweet! Tweet!" "It'll be along soon," they said, trying hard to comfort the sobbing Katya. But the starling did not appear. "Well, this is no good," said Tanya at last. "We'll have to stick up a notice." She ran up to a student sitting under a linden tree solving a mathematical problem, and asked him for a sheet of paper. While he was tearing it

out of his exercise book she managed to explain the situation
to him, and the student kindly lent her a big pencil that wrote
in blue and red. Tanya wrote in large red and blue letters:

Then they hung the notice up on the biggest tree they could
find in the avenue.

"We'd better split up and go and look in different places,"
said Lilia.

"Who goes where?" asked Shura.

"I'll take charge," announced Tanya. "First let's draw lots.
Right, Katya?" Katya merely nodded. She was ready to agree
to anything provided the starling was found.

"Avenue for me!" said Shura.

"Yards for me!" cried Lilia. "Worse luck!"

"Park for me!" said Katya sadly.

"And the hardest for me! S. and F., Square and Fountain!"
announced Tanya, and added confidently, "Never mind, we'll
find it somehow." And so the girls split up.

Poor Katya made her way down the little path through the
park. She had no hope whatever of finding anything. She
walked on, her head bent, sobbing bitterly, leaving little drops
in her path that made it look as though it had been raining.

There was nothing to be done. Best go home. She went up the stairs, half-running, half-dragging her feet. One moment she would hope that somehow all the animals had turned up and were waiting for her at home. The next moment she would pause, scared of discovering that, as before, there was still no trace of them.

At home, there was only the crocodile. Katya glanced at it and then turned away. Grandmother tried not to look at her – she was afraid she might burst into tears. Katya went and huddled on a corner of the divan and waited in terror for the doorbell to ring. And ring it did. Long, loud and piercing. But she dared not go and open it lest it was Mitya come for the animals.

Milka burst into the room with the macaroni boy – Milka panting after her chase and the lad quite dry after his bathe. *The tortoise was with them!* Katya laughed for joy. For a moment it seemed that things were not so bad after all. But only for a moment. Neither the rabbits nor the starling had turned up yet. "The crocodile is the most important," said Father calmly. "You can always get hold of a rabbit or a starling."

Just then Puss, returning from a long walk, looked lazily in through the window from the outside ledge. Suddenly it bent its head, its whiskers twitched greedily, and with an immense leap it hurtled into the room past Father, nearly knocking him off his feet, flung itself into the cupboard and disappeared. Father gave a start. "What, you again!" he exclaimed. Inside the cupboard a terrific racket ensued. The door swung open, and out flew a white ball which separated into cat and rabbit.

"Ah!" screamed Katya, and pressed the rabbit tight in her arms. But then she suddenly grew scared in case she might damage it, so she put it in the hutch.

"Now what do you say to that!" beamed Grandmother. "That is most certainly my rabbit."

"I beg your pardon," objected Father, to whom something else was now becoming clearer, "it's *my* rabbit." But whether it was his or Grandmother's, it was certainly time to give it something to eat. Katya poured out a quantity of oatmeal and

Grandmother brought some cabbage leaves in from the kitchen. Then she started bustling around, opening all the cupboards and drawers in the flat. But *her* rabbit was not to be found. And Puss, having once again realized that it hadn't caught a mouse, got moody and went out through the window.

Then there was a ring, a very gentle one – though to Katya's ears it sounded more like a rumble of thunder. "It's too late," she whispered to herself, "this must be him." And she clasped her hands very tightly together. She stood up. She could already see Mitya coming in, holding the dreaded receipt in his hands with the fateful words: "I promise to return the school property safe and intact." She clenched her fists and whispered: "I have not protected the school property." There was another ring. Grandma rushed towards Katya. "It was all my fault, silly ninny that I am. Don't cry, Katya dear, I will tell him myself . . ."

Shaking his head and sighing, Father went to the front door. Milka crept under the bed in terror. Father opened the door. "Ah it's you, Sasha," he said happily. "Well done, Sasha Medvedkin!"

Sasha, neat and tidy, came in, cleared his throat and said almost in a whisper: "Very many thanks. From Mother. And from Father. And from me."

"You haven't pipped your exam?" asked Mr Pastushkov.

"No! I got Excellent!" he beamed. "That's because you made me practise three hours every day!"

"Well, well," said Father. "Let me congratulate my pupil of the College of Music and the future first violin of our Philharmonic Orchestra!" They all laughed.

"Thank you," said Sasha. "Mother, Father and I would be very happy if you would accept this modest . . . er . . . er . . . with cream!" And from behind his back he pulled out a large cake-box.

"Well, well, my boy," said Father, rather embarrassed.

Sasha thrust the box into Father's hands and ran out through the door, shouting from the stairs: "Thank you very much!"

Father came back into the room where the others were sitting in silence. "You never know who is likely to turn up," he said gaily. "Meanwhile, let's have a few plates and a large knife."

"And some for me, over here," announced Milka, from under the bed.

Grandmother quickly set out some plates and Father cut the tape and raised the lid. Out of the box, complete with cotton-wool, sprang a white rabbit – right on to the table-cloth. "I don't believe it," said Father, and sat down, nearly missing the chair.

The starling was feeling thirsty. From up aloft it spied a fountain, and down it flew to perch on the head of the marble statue. "Hullo," it chirped gaily.

"That's the one! It talks! That's the one the notice is about! Catch it! Catch it!" came shouts from all directions. Katya's friends set up a whoop of delight. A whole crowd of people made a mad rush for the fountain. The frightened starling whisked its tail and flew up over the square without having managed to quench its thirst. And after it, stamping and fingers pointing, came children and grown-ups, running and shouting.

184

The starling got away just in time. It started to dart in and out among the roof-tops and settled down at last on the highest television aerial. Once more it felt thirsty and in the gutter of the roof it caught sight of a little rusty water. Down it fluttered and was seen by Grandmother's white cat as it strolled along the roof. It hadn't read the notice, but it, too, was on the look out for the starling. Up it sneaked and gave a spring. The starling darted away. Outstretched claws grazed its tail. . . . It swooped forward like an arrow and flew into the first open window.

So once more, Puss was unlucky, its prey had given it the slip. Trying hard to maintain its dignity, the cat sloped off.

Meanwhile, what had Mitya been doing all this time? He had had a brilliant idea. If the animals were to be entrusted to anyone, Volodya was the best person. So now Mitya was speeding along in the electric train to the small station in the village of Martushkin where his friend Volodya lived.

Mitya had found Volodya pumping a tyre at the back of a large shed. On the walls hung a bow, a quiver of arrows, a spare wheel and a toy pistol. The sun pierced a chink in the wall, and a beam fell on an old barrel full of green water; on the surface floated – as though on skis – a long-legged water-fly. In one corner stood a pair of roller skates and a fishing rod; in another lay some hay. "Oh, hullo, it's you!" said Volodya, delighted to see his friend. "This is my work-room. Jolly good, don't you think?"

Mitya nodded and sighed with relief. There was certainly enough space for his entire menagerie here. And he proceeded to tell Volodya the whole story.

Volodya listened in silence and knitted his brows. "Idiot!" he said.

"Why idiot?" asked Mitya,

"Because you *are* an idiot, that's why," said Volodya.

"You will take them, though, won't you?" Mitya's voice was rather subdued.

"Take what?"

185

"The animals."

Volodya fixed his friend with a devastating look. "You're too late! I bet your animals have already vanished. Fancy giving them to someone you don't even know! You might as well have drowned them yourself right away!"

"But I've got a receipt," mumbled Mitya, producing a piece of paper.

"Fat lot of good that'll be!" said Volodya.

Mitya turned pale. Then they looked at one another and as though by some secret agreement they made for the station.

With gathering speed the train came puffing out of Martushkin towards the town. Volodya and Mitya sat in silence, but Volodya was beginning to feel a bit sorry for Mitya. He said: "Do you know what? I know a little creek down by the sea. If we could partition it off we could build a first-class swimming pool for the crocodile. What do you think?" Mitya looked at him. Did that mean there was still hope?

There was a ring at Katya's door. "It wouldn't surprise me if it was the starling complete with top hat and walking stick," said Father.

Grandmother went out to open the door while Katya listened anxiously. "Is Katherine Pastushkov in?" It was Mitya's voice. Katya began to tremble and Milka again sought refuge under the bed. As she saw the two boys come in through the doorway, Katya felt her mouth was too parched to greet them. She didn't have the strength to say, "Hullo."

"Hullo," came from behind her back. She spun round; there in its cage was the starling. It was fluttering its wings over the water and splashing all over the place.

"Hullo, boys," said Katya in clear ringing tones.

The boys anxiously switched their gaze from the tortoise to the rabbits, from the rabbits to the crocodile, and from the crocodile to the starling. Then they smiled. "Hullo," they replied politely, and in unison. Father was sitting on the divan, enjoying the situation immensely. "I hope our animals haven't been too much trouble," Mitya enquired rather formally.

"No, of course not! Not at all!" everybody answered at once and Father added: "If ever you need to leave . . . say an elephant, for example, or a tiger or . . . well, don't hesitate. They'll all be welcome."

Mitya drew out the receipt, very business-like. He read: "Angora rabbits – two."

"Right," cried Katya and handed the hutch to Volodya.

"European tortoise – one."

"One," said Katya and Milka together.

"Madagascar Crocodile – one. Talking starling – one." Volodya covered the cage with a handkerchief. "That's the lot," concluded Mitya and pushed down the lid of the croquet case.

"You should have seen it in the drainpipe," said the macaroni boy suddenly with a laugh, and nearly ruined everything.

"O.K., then, that's fine!" put in Father hastily, signalling to him to be quiet, and the boy lapsed into silence.

Mitya and Volodya went up to Katya and each in turn shook her hand. Then they bowed to Father, to Grandmother and even to Milka. "Goodbye," they said.

Just then the cat appeared at the window. "Not taking him?" asked Father, pointing to Puss.

"No, not the cat," replied the boys seriously. Then the bell rang again.

"Very interesting," said Father. "Wonder who it can be this time. This has certainly been a day for callers." He opened the door, and there stood Alexander Ivanovitch Medvedkin, holding an enormous cake-box in his hands. "Now look here," said Father, taking him by the lapel of his jacket. "Tell me the truth. How did you get our rabbit?"

"What rabbit?" asked Mr Medvedkin.

Father looked intently into his honest, wondering eyes and realized that Mr Medvedkin really knew nothing whatsoever about the rabbit. And that was a fact. Having been run off his feet with work at the office he hadn't sent the cake home.

And when he did get back, neither his wife nor his son was in the house; they had gone to the cinema. So he himself took the cake to the Pastushkovs.

"It's a good thing there are still some mysteries left in this world," said Father, closing the door after Mr Medvedkin. He strode back into the room and declared: "If this really and truly is a cake and not an electric eel or a wolf-cub, we are going to eat it now." Grandmother made everyone sit down at the table. Father armed himself with a knife, but before cutting the ribbon he bent over the box and listened carefully. Inside all was peaceful. He then carefully cut the ribbon and raised the lid. Inside was a beautiful cream cake decorated with yellow roses and lovely chocolate fishes.

"Well, I think I'll be off now," observed the macaroni boy suddenly, quite out of the blue, and to everybody's great surprise. They tried to persuade him to stay. "No!" said the lad firmly, picking up his bag. "Mother told me to be back home in ten minutes with the macaroni. I think I've been a bit longer than that."

He glanced out of the window.

Along the street the lamps were beginning to light up.

ACKNOWLEDGEMENTS

We are grateful to the undermentioned authors and publishers for permission to include the following material:

"Sam Becomes a Ghost" from *Our Sam, the Daftest Dog in the World* by John Cunliffe and "The Flood" from *Ten Tales of Shellover* by Ruth Ainsworth, published by André Deutsch Ltd.

"Arabel's Raven" from *Tales of Arabel's Raven* by Joan Aiken, published by Jonathan Cape Ltd, minimally abridged with the generous permission of the author; and "Lob's Girl" by Joan Aiken, reprinted by permission of the author and A M Heath & Co Ltd.

"Zlateh The Goat" from *Zlateh The Goat and Other Stories* by Isaac Bashevis Singer, translated from the Yiddish by the Author and Elizabeth Shub. Text copyright © 1966 Isaac Bashevis Singer. Reprinted by Harper and Row, Publishers Inc.

"Chut the Kangaroo" from *Wilderness Orphan* by Dorothy Cottrell. Reprinted by permission of Paul R Reynolds Inc.

"Juju the Jackdaw" by Hazel Wilkinson, copyright Hazel Wilkinson 1984.

"The Christmas Cat" by Adèle Geras, and "The Amazing Pet" by Marjorie Newman, published by Hamish Hamilton Ltd.

189

Acknowledgements

"A Pet for Mrs Arbuckle" by Gwenda Smyth, first published by Thomas Nelson Australia and published in Great Britain by Hamish Hamilton Ltd.

"The Great Hamster Hunt" by Lenore and Erik Blegvad, reprinted by permission of William Heinemann Ltd.

"The Great Hamster Hunt", text copyright © 1969 by Lenore Blegvad, is reprinted by permission of Harcourt Brace Jovanovich, Inc.

"Wol Helps Out" from *Owls in the Family* by Farley Mowat, by permission of Macmillan, London and Basingstoke, and by permission of the Canadian Publishers, McClelland and Stewart Ltd, Toronto.

For their ever-ready help we should like to thank the following Schools Librarians: for Barnet, Mary Junor, for Redbridge, Christine Pountney, for Birmingham, Vivien Griffiths, and for East Herts, Janet Hill; also Grace McElwee and Angela Duckering, Children's Librarians for the Borough of Camden, Joan Ludford and Helen Williams, Children's Librarians, Letchworth; and the Children's Librarians in the Barnet Libraries.

To Phyllis Hunt, our Editor at Fabers, and to Juliet Gardner, it is difficult to express our gratitude for constant advice, suggestions and guidance all the way through.